D1282997

THE SEVENTH-DAY ADVENTISTS

THE SEVENTH-DAY ADVENTISTS

A History

Anne Devereaux Jordan

HIPPOCRENE BOOKS
New York

Unless otherwise indicated, scripture quotations taken from *The Holy Bible*, King James Version.

For information, address: Hippocrene Books, Inc.,
171 Madison Avenue, New York, NY 10016.

Library of Congress Cataloging-in-Publication Data

Jordan, Anne Devereaux.
The Seventh-Day Adventists : a history / Anne Devereaux Jordan.
p. 180 31½ × 47 cm.
Bibliography: p. 169
Includes index.
ISBN 0-87052-562-X:
1. Seventh-Day Adventists—History. 2. Adventists—History.
3. Sabbatarains—History. I. Title.
BX6153.J67 1988 88-16562
286.7'32'09—dc19 CIP

Printed in the United States of America.

For David,
and for Francelia

Acknowledgments

Grateful acknowledgment is made for permission to quote from the following sources:

Excerpts from: *Origin and History of Seventh-day Adventists*, volumes 1, 2, and 3, by Arthur W. Spalding © 1961, 1962 by the Review and Herald Publishing Association; *The Great Advent Movement* by Emma Howell Cooper © 1935 by the Review and Herald Publishing Association. *The Story of the Seventh-day Adventists* by Eugene F. Durand © 1968 by the Review and Herald Publishing Association; *Seventh-day Adventist Yearbook, 1987,* © 1987 by the Review and Herald Publishing Association; *The Story of Our Health Message,* by D. E. Robinson, © 1965 by the Southern Publishing Association. Excerpts reprinted by permission of the Review and Herald Publishing Association.

Excerpts from: *Tell It to the World* by C. Mervyn Maxwell © 1976, by Pacific Press Publishing Association; *Testimonies for the Church*, volume 1, 7 and 8 © 1948 by Ellen G. White Publications; *Testimony Treasures*, volumes 1, 2, and 3, ©

1949 by Ellen G. White Publications; *A Century of Miracles* by Richard Utt © 1963 by Pacific Press Publishing Association; *Legacy: The Heritage of a Unique International Medical Outreach* by Richard A. Schaefer, © 1978 by Richard A. Schaefer; *How to Survive the '80's* by Lewis R. Walton and Herbert E. Douglass, © 1982 by Pacific Press Publishing Association. Excerpts reprinted by permission of the Pacific Press Publishing Association, Ellen G. White Publications and Richard A. Schaefer.

Excerpts from *A Synopsis of American History* by Charles Sellers and Henry May © 1963 by Rand McNally and Company. Excerpts reprinted by permission of Rand McNally and Company.

Excerpts from: *Then Was the Future: The North in the Age of Jackson, 1815–1850* by Douglas T. Miller © 1973 by Douglas T. Miller; *For Jefferson and Liberty: The United States in War and Peace, 1800–1815* by Leonard Falkner © 1972 by Leonard Falkner. Excerpts reprinted by permission of the authors and Alfred A. Knopf Incorporated.

Excerpts from *Eyewitness: The Negro in American History* by William L. Katz © 1968 by Pitman Publishing Incorporated. Excerpts reprinted by permission of Pitman Publishing Incorporated.

Excerpts from *American Manners and Morals* by Mary Cable *et al.*, editors, © 1969 by American Heritage Publishing Company. Excerpts reprinted by permission of American Heritage Publishing Company.

I am also grateful to Mr. and Mrs. George Sands, Richard Schaefer and James Haskins for their assistance, and, of course, to Bob Crouse for his help and support.

Contents

About the Seventh-day Adventists

THE SEVENTH-DAY ADVENTISTS WERE ORGANIZED AS A union of existing Adventist sects in 1863 by Ellen Harmon White and her husband, James White. The name "Seventh-day Adventists" derives from the belief that Saturday, the seventh day of the week according to Genesis 2:1–3 and Exodus 20:8–11, is the sabbath, and from their belief in the Second Coming of Christ. The Seventh-day Adventists follow the Bible strictly. They practice baptism by immersion. Children are baptized when they are considered old enough to understand the significance of the ceremony. Foot washing precedes communion services which are held once every quarter and on special occasions.

Many Seventh-day Adventists practice vegetarianism and all refrain from eating pork. Tobacco, alcohol and other drugs (except those prescribed by a physician) are not used. The Seventh-day Adventist Church maintains extensive medical-aid, publishing and missionary programs around the world. As of 1986, the Seventh-day Adventist Church had a world-wide membership of nearly five million.

I

"Go Ahead"

IN 1795 A YOUNG IRISHMAN NAMED ISAAC WELD TRAVeled to the United States with his manservant to "establish the truth of various accounts of the flourishing and happy condition of the United States of America."[1] As his ship approached the coastline, he saw wilderness.

> The first objects which meet the eye on approaching the American coast are the tops of trees which thickly cover the shore to the water's edge. At last the tall forest rising out of the ocean presents itself in all its majesty.[2]

The United States had just weathered the storm for independence. What Weld saw from his ship on approaching this new country was the same thing settlers coming from other countries saw. It was wilderness, yes, but full of resources, full of opportunity. The wilderness was, within a few, short decades, to be beaten back, allowing a great and busy nation to emerge.

Only twenty-nine years after Weld's arrival, Daniel Webster, the noted Massachusetts lawyer, was to write:

> There has been in the course of half a century an unprecedented augmentation of general wealth. Even within a shorter period, and under the actual observation of most of us, in our own country and our own circles, vastly increased comforts have come to be enjoyed by the industrious classes, and vastly more leisure and time are found for the cultivation of the mind. . . . We may safely take the fact to be, as it certainly is, that there are certain causes which have acted with peculiar energy in our generation, and which have improved the condition of the mass of society with a degree of rapidity heretofore altogether unknown. . . .[3]

The cause for this rapid change, Daniel Webster wrote, was "the application of science to art"—invention. Steam power had revolutionized the country, allowed ease in travel, and quickly was being adapted for the powering of machinery in manufacturing and industry. Change in all areas was rapid, on both a technological and a personal level.

"The first thing which strikes a traveler in the United States is the innumerable multitude of those who seek to throw off their original condition," wrote a visitor to this country.

> No Americans are devoid of a yearning desire to rise. . . . It is not only a portion of the people which is busied with the amelioration of its social condition, but the whole community is engaged in the task.[4]

While the majority applauded this rapid change in lifestyle and social status, others deplored it. For them change was coming *too* quickly. "We have become the most careless, reckless, headlong people on the face of the earth," gentleman and diarist Philip Hone lamented in 1830. "'Go Ahead' is our maxim and password. . . ."[5]

In 1806 the Lewis and Clark Expedition returned from the West and in 1826 the Erie Canal was completed. The nation could now "go ahead" to the newly opened frontiers. There was a flood of people and commerce westward. With the introduction of steam power and its application to manufacturing, businesses could now "go ahead" with industrial expansion. Likewise, there seemed to be a rush to "go ahead" in new amusements, manners, morals, and social standards. With the 1830s came the development of the two-party political system. For many this created the opportunity to "go ahead" in politics.

While many lauded these advances and changes, others were frightened by them. Their beliefs were being undermined or overthrown altogether by the determination of the growing country. The pursuit of money and success was pushing aside the more down-to-earth virtues, and the faster this was done, the better, many felt. A man who had settled in the United States in the 1820s wrote:

> The Americans seem to know no greater pleasure than that of going on fast, and accomplishing large distances in comparatively short times. . . . This continual motion of the Americans . . . resembles, on a huge scale, the vibrations of a pendulum. . . . This state of incessant excitement gives to the American an air of busy inquietude . . . which, in fact constitutes their principle happiness.[6]

And unhappiness.

Many of the citizens of the young United States were seriously worried about the effects all this change and "excitement" were having on the nation's moral and religious character. As early as 1818 the effect seemed to be a negative one. A New Englander visiting Virginia in that year wrote that

> too few regard the sabbath, except as a holiday; or wherein to begin or end a journey. In some places, toward Norwalk, shops are kept open, only the buyer may walk round to the side door to evade the law. . . . The ancient Episcopal churches which once were so predominant are mostly in a state of delapidation. The rank reeds rustle round their doors; the fox looks out their windows. . . .[7]

Religion seemed to be dying beneath the wheels of progress and commerce. Many felt that the changing character and composition of the citizens of the United

States was having a bad influence on its overall national character.

In the 1800s, the United States was viewed as a land of opportunity. A flood of immigrants surged to its shores. They sought freedom and wealth, looking for the fabled "streets paved with gold." Between 1830 and 1840 alone, half a million immigrants arrived in America.[8] Increasingly, however, these people met with ill-will as they arrived. Many of those already settled in the United States did not want the world's poor and oppressed "dumped" on them. The only results of such an influx, they felt, would be disease, filth, poverty, and a corruption of beliefs. Many of the immigrants were of the Catholic faith. Too often the thrifty Protestant Yankees already here felt there was a definite plot to bring Catholicism to America and subvert the government to the aims of that faith and the dictates of the Pope.

In reaction the "Know-Nothing" party was born in the 1830s. It was an antiforeigner, anti-Catholic movement. Although many members of the Know-Nothing party did indeed know nothing, it also included some intelligent, educated citizens who viewed the changes in America with fear. Samuel F.B. Morse, the inventor of the telegraph, wrote a pamphlet in 1835 calling to his fellow citizens to defend themselves against a Papist conspiracy to be brought about by all the immigrants. "Up! up! I beseech you. Awake!" he wrote, "To your posts! Let the tocsin sound from Maine to Louisiana!"[9] Morse and the Know-Nothing party urged stricter immigration laws to stem the tide of what they saw as

Catholic corruption from abroad and to maintain the "purity" of the United States.

While Morse and others fought to protect America from outside threats, others fought a threat from within. At the turn of the nineteenth century, the United States slowly was being pulled in two directions. One direction seemed to offer freedom from oppression to the immigrants arriving on its shores; from the other, it harbored that "peculiar institution"—slavery. It held out a lure of education and freedom from religious persecution, yet denied those same things to a multitude of people already living in the country. White ministers preached to black slaves that they always must obey their masters. In the South black slaves struggled to obtain any kind of education. One slave recalled, "My father and other boys used to crawl under the house an' lie on the ground to hear massa read the newspaper to missus."[10]

These dichotomous attitudes of change versus stability, freedom versus slavery, and others, had a weakening effect upon many in the United States. The American Revolution had brought with it the spiritual and moral laxity usual in wartime. Change and contradiction had added to this, and many felt there were no longer any guidelines upon which to build their lives. A great number drew upon the Enlightenment of the eighteenth century and turned to Deism for an explanation of this seemingly chaotic world.

Deism is a belief based upon reason that states that God, having created the world and the universe and set them in motion, then abandoned them. Having abandoned the universe, God assumed no control over a person's life, set no guidelines, and exerted no influence. An individual was left alone to direct his or her own life.

While Deists felt God had left them alone, others kept the form and language of the traditional churches but came to believe in a reasonable, not wrathful, God who was favorably disposed toward man. This idea set aside the earlier puritanical notion of an angry God ready to punish sin. Those who accepted a reasonable God felt man was reasonable enough himself to be capable of goodness. They believed that the goal was goodness in this world rather than salvation in a world to come.

Faced with these beliefs in the first decade of the nineteenth century, the orthodox clergy resorted to the vigorous, emotional counteroffensive known as the Great Revival to bring people back to their churches. The Great Revival and its effects lasted for more than twenty-five years. It wiped out all traces of Deism and gave rise to a number of new religions.

The Great Revival centered around the camp meeting and was most effective along the new frontiers of the United States. It provided a release of pent-up emotion and an element of entertainment for many frontier folk. The camp meeting gave them something to look forward to besides lonely days in isolated cabins.

> Methodists predominated, with a sprinkling of Baptists and Presbyterians. Sometimes as many as twenty thousand people gathered from a hundred-mile radius, camping in the woods in family groups from a Friday to a Tuesday, and listening to sermons morning, noon, and night. Each meeting reached a crescendo of excitement, at which point hysteria generally broke out and the congregation

> was prone to twitch, jerk, leap, shout, sob and emit an eerie sound called the Holy Laugh. Those who believed themselves repentant came forward and fell on their knees.[11]

Crowds would follow the preacher's words, calling out "amen!" "yes, Lord," "hallelujah!" or making barking noises that were supposed to "tree the Devil."

The furor of the Great Revival died down after its first explosive glory, but it left behind an enthusiasm for religion ready to be organized. Those in the camp meetings who were charged by the idea of salvation looked to other means to achieve this salvation and perfection in this world, to gain the stable base they sought in this "go ahead" society.

Many Utopian groups were founded in an attempt to create a perfect community on earth. These communities emphasized love and the freedom from sin that comes with salvation. The Mormons and the Shakers were two communities of believers born from the Great Revival. While many of the communities were condemned as immoral by the general public and died out, others, such as the Mormons, survived criticism and eventually gained respectability and acceptance in the eyes of nonbelievers.

The Great Revival also inspired a broader series of movements aimed at wiping out the evils of the age. Many of these movements were millennial; the adherents believed that the millennium was soon to come and Christ soon would return to this world. Christ would then establish a heavenly kingdom on this earth. This belief was based on interpretation of various passages in the Bible that seemed to describe the events of the 1800s and predict Christ's return.

One of the most persuasive and forceful of the millennial movements was that led by William Miller of New York State, who was himself a former Deist. His belief in the advent of Christ developed in the 1830s, when the young country seemed most in turmoil and the "go ahead" philosophy seemed most in conflict with the desire to live a moral life. The sincere Miller offered his followers hope and salvation of a real kind. The Great Revival had been fleeting and, for many, disillusioning. William Miller restored the faith many had thought lost with the dying flame of the Great Revival.

II

Faith and Failure: The Millerites

WILLIAM MILLER WAS BORN IN 1782 IN LOW HAMPTON, New York, a rural region of lakes, rolling hills, and farms in the upper part of New York State. His childhood was normal for a boy growing up on a farm: long working hours, care for crops and animals, and Sundays spent with his family at the Baptist church in the nearby village. The only thing that set Miller apart from his peers was that he was a voracious reader.

William Miller was an eloquent and persuasive speaker.

> His manner of preaching was not flowery or oratorical, but he dealt in plain and startling facts that roused his hearers from their careless indif-

> ference. He supported his statements and theories by Scripture proof as he progressed. A convincing power attended his words that seemed to stamp them as the language of truth.[1]

What Miller spoke of, moving his listeners from indifference to enthusiasm, was the Second Coming of Christ, which he said would happen within the lifetime of his audience.

In an age and area where most people were farmers, Miller also became a farmer. In 1803 he married and moved to Poultney, Vermont, in the Green Mountains. Helped by his wife, Lucy, Miller still found time to read, and quickly exhausted the local library.[2] Miller read the writings of David Hume, Voltaire, and Thomas Paine. He sought answers to the seeming contradictions between what existed in the world and what was pronounced in the Bible. As a result of his reading, he turned to Deism as the only logical explanation of the world, despite the urging of his mother to return to the Baptist beliefs in which he had been raised. He felt that what one achieved in this life was what mattered and that the hope for man lay in supporting the struggling young country. His home became a meetingplace for others who shared his views. He spoke to them as convincingly in support of Deism and love of country as he later spoke fervently in support of adventism.

Believing as he did that hope lay in aiding the United States, Miller volunteered for service in the War of 1812. Forty-seven others volunteered with him on the condition that they serve directly under his command.[3]

The War of 1812 is generally considered by historians to be one of America's mistakes. Feeling threatened by the British and Spanish, and having a desire to gain Canada and Florida as territories, the United States rushed into war without thought or preparation. Except for the fact that the British already were occupied in fighting Napoleon, the War of 1812 would have been a total disaster. As it was, one invading British army easily captured the city of Washington, D.C., and burned the public buildings before withdrawing.[4] The only significant victories for the Americans were the Battle of Plattsburg and the Battle of New Orleans, the latter occurring after the war had officially ended. The Battle of Plattsburg was fought on the shores of Lake Champlain in New York State, not far from William Miller's boyhood home. Miller and his men were ordered to the shores of the lake and there fought bravely in this one American triumph.

"Sir: It is over, it is done," Miller wrote to his commanding officer on September 11, 1814, the afternoon of the battle.

> The British fleet has struck to the American flag. Great slaughter on both sides—they are in plain view, where I am now writing. . . . The sight was majestic, it was noble, it was grand. This morning, at ten o'clock the British opened a very heavy and destructive fire upon us, both by water and land. Their . . . rockets flew like hailstones. . . . You have no idea of the battle. . . . You must conceive what we feel, for I cannot describe it.[5]

In December of 1814 the British and Americans met at Ghent in Belgium and agreed upon a treaty, although the fighting continued into 1815 with Andrew Jackson's defeat of the British at New Orleans in January. Historians concede that the battles of Plattsburg and New Orleans played significant roles in the treaty negotiations and that, had the Americans lost those battles, the British would have insisted upon concessions from the United States before ratifying the treaty. The victories demonstrated to the British America's strength.

Miller returned home from the war in victory in 1815. The rashness of the war, however, and the improbability of the victory at Plattsburg made him question the basis of his Deistic beliefs. It seemed as if God had taken a hand in aiding the American side. But if this were so, reasoned Miller, then God had not abandoned the world. He was not the "watch-maker" of Deistic tradition who, having wound up and set the world in motion like a clock, then left it to run alone. Being the reader he was, Miller once again turned to books, and to the Bible, to help him resolve his dilemma. "From 1816 to 1822 he continued to study, testing his conclusions against all possible objections, before writing out his 1822 statement of faith. . . ."[6]

During this period Miller and his family moved back to Low Hampton. His father had died and Miller paid the mortgage on his boyhood home for his mother and settled on a 200-acre farm nearby. At the urging of his mother and his uncle, a Baptist minister, he renewed his attendance at the local Baptist church whenever his uncle gave the sermon. These encounters with the Baptist church and with religion focused the attention of Miller's studies more and more upon the Bible. He found himself particularly intrigued by a text in the Old Testament book of Daniel.

> The one said, "For how long will the period of this vision last? How long will the regular offering be suppressed, how long will impiety cause desolation, and both the Holy Place and the fairest of all lands be given over to be trodden down?" The answer came, "For two thousand three hundred evenings and mornings; then the Holy Place shall emerge victorious" (Daniel 8:13–14).

The passage in Daniel set Miller thinking. In 1818 he came to the conclusion that, based upon that text, Christ would return "about the year 1843," the 2300 days mentioned in Daniel having passed, according to his calculations, and "in about twenty-five years . . . all the affairs of our present state would be wound up."[7] This doctrine of a "temporal" millennium—a period when sin would be eliminated, the world evangelized, and universal happiness would prevail—was not a new one. Writers in Britain and continental Europe, as well as North America, had reached similar conclusions. The most popular dates set for the millennium were 1843, 1844, and 1847, though some looked to 1866 or 1867.[8] The energy behind the predictions of these writers had died out quickly, however, unlike the enthusiasm Miller was to generate with his prophecies.

It was not until 1831 that Miller felt called upon to spread word of his discovery, but he was reluctant to do so. He was only a farmer, then about fifty years old, with no experience in public speaking. He was used to discussing his views with small groups of friends, not with strangers. According to various accounts, Miller finally promised the Lord that he would speak publicly on his views but only if he were invited to do so.

> Within a half an hour came Miller's sister's boy, Irving Guilford, who lived about sixteen miles away [to ask him to preach]. . . . When the request came, Miller's heart quailed, but there was nothing he could do but fulfill his promise to the Lord.[9]

Miller spoke on his ideas of the Second Coming of Christ. Word spread about these ideas and he received more and more invitations to speak. "In 1833 a local Baptist who knew Miller well signed a license for him to preach."[10] Miller, although not ordained, was now licensed to speak and to spread what he felt was the truth. More and more of the crowds to whom he spoke became convinced of his views and soon took to calling themselves "Millerites."

On November 13, 1833, an event occurred that seemed to confirm Miller's predictions. In the Book of Matthew (24:29), Christ prophesied that "Immediately after the tribulation of those days shall the sun be darkened and the moon shall not give her light, and the stars shall fall from heaven and the powers of the heavens shall be shaken." In 1833 there was a meteor shower later described by astronomer W.J. Fisher in 1934 as "the most magnificent meteor shower on record."[11] In 1876 R.M. Devens called it astounding. He had observed it from the edge of Niagara Falls and wrote that ". . .an incessant play of dazzlingly brilliant luminosities was kept up in the whole heavens. Some of these were of great magnitude and most peculiar form. . . . the first appearance was that of fireworks of the most imposing grandeur, covering the entire vault of heaven with myriads of fire-balls resembling sky-rockets. . . . no spectacle so terribly grand and sublime was ever before beheld by man as that of the firmament descending in fiery torrents over the dark and roaring cataract."[12] He continues on to note that "Arago computes that not less than two hundred and forty thousand meteors were at the same time visible above the horizon of Boston."[13]

For the Millerites the meteor shower seemed the second sign of the imminent arrival of Christ. The first sign, they felt, was a "darkening of the sun" that had occurred on May 19, 1780. On that day an eclipse occurred that began between 10 and 11 A.M. and lasted approximately fifteen hours.[14] This "darkening," combined with the falling of the stars in 1833, convinced Miller and his followers that the Advent of Christ was near.

The Millerite movement was regarded as harmless by most traditional clergy, especially as William Miller urged his listeners to remain with their own churches and his following was small. By 1840 Miller actually included a number of prominent ministers of the time among his followers. The most influential of them, to Miller, was Joseph V. Himes. He urged Miller to shift from preaching in small, rural areas to preaching in cities so he could reach more people. Himes took over the promotion of Miller's views, and organized and promoted Miller's movement.

Himes was born in 1805 and was trained as a cabinet-maker. In 1827 he became a minister of the Christian Connection and organized the Second Christian Church of Boston.[15] Joseph Himes proved to be just the campaign manager Miller needed. He organized other ministers to preach and spread Miller's ideas and launched and edited the Adventist periodical, *Signs of the Times*. *Signs of the Times* was soon imitated in other cities by other followers of Miller, resulting in the publication of *Midnight Cry, Glad Tidings, Advent Chronicle, Jubilee Trumpet, Philadelphia Alarm* and many others. Miller's word was spreading.

By 1843 the traditional clergy was becoming concerned about the popularity of the Millerite movement. At a meeting of Methodist ministers that year, a resolution opposing the Advent doctrine was passed. It was typical of the reaction of many churches.

> *Resolved*, That the peculiarities of that theory relative to the second coming of Christ and the end of the world, denominated Millerism, together with all its modifications, are contrary to the standards of the church, and we are constrained to regard them as among the erroneous and strange doctrines which we are pledged to banish and drive away.[16]

The traditional clergy openly opposed Millerism and banished members of their churches who espoused it. They were even more outraged, however, when Miller, at the urging of his followers, set an actual time for the Second Coming of Christ: spring of 1844.

When Miller first started preaching the Second Advent he set no definite date. As he continued preaching, however, he was urged by his listeners to tell them when Christ would come. Using 457 B.C., Miller's calculation of the time when Daniel wrote his prophecies, as a starting date, he calculated: 457 B.C. + 2300 years = 1843–1844. Using the rabbinical Jewish calendar as a reference, he said

> I am fully convinced that sometime between March 21st, 1843 and March 21st, 1844 [the Jewish year], according to the Jewish Mode of computation of time, Christ will come.[17]

But April 1844 passed and the Second Advent had not occurred. Many Millerites turned against the movement because of this, but others, most notably Charles Fitch, Apollos Hale, Sylvester Bliss, and Samuel S. Snow, determined that an error had been made in their figuring. They pointed out that the biblical parable of the wise and foolish virgins (Matthew 25:1–13) indicated there would be a delay, a "tarrying time." Christ would return to this world, and soon, but they had yet to determine the new time.

In the meantime opposition to the Millerite movement was coming to a head. The traditional churches rejected Miller's predictions and told Miller's followers that they must renounce his views or leave their churches. In the summer of 1844, Joseph V. Himes wrote

> Most of them [the believers] loved their churches, and could not think of leaving. But when they were ridiculed, oppressed, and in various ways cut off from their former privileges and enjoyments, and when the "meat in due season" was withheld from them, and the syren song of "peace and safety" was sounded in their ears from Sabbath to

> Sabbath, they were soon weaned from their party predilections, and arose in the majesty of their strength, shook off the yoke, and raised the cry, "Come out of her my people."[18]

Miller was condemned in other quarters as well. Noted lexicographer Noah Webster wrote to Miller

> Your preaching can be of no use to society but it is a great annoyance. If you expect to frighten men and women into religion, you are probably mistaken. . . . If your preaching drives people into despair or insanity, you are responsible for the consequences. I advise you to abandon your preaching; you are doing no good, but you may do a great deal of harm.[19]

A great number of Miller's followers ignored the criticisms against him, as did Miller himself. They left their churches but did not organize a new church. They felt that there was no need to do so since the Second Coming of Christ was so close at hand and it would go against Miller's announcements that it was not his intention to organize a new religious denomination. Miller's followers were united as never before by the criticisms and by the thought that the time of Christ's return was near.

On October 6th, 1844, Miller wrote, "If Christ does not come within twenty or twenty-five days, I shall feel twice the disappointment I did in the spring."[20] Finally, Miller set a second date for the advent: October 22, 1844. This, Miller and his followers felt, was the *true* date; the "tarrying time" was over.

On October 11, Miller wrote to Himes,

> I think I have never seen among our brethren such *faith* as is manifested in the seventh month. "He will come," is the common expression. "He will not tarry the second time," is their general reply. There is a forsaking of the world, an unconcern for the wants of life, a general searching of heart, confession of sin, and a deep feeling in prayer for Christ to come. A preparation of heart to meet Him seems to be the labor of their agonizing spirits. There is something in this present waking up different from anything I have ever before seen. There is no great expression of joy: that is, as it were, suppressed for a future occasion, when all heaven and earth will rejoice together with joy unspeakable and full of glory. There is no shouting; that, too, is reserved for the shout from heaven. . . . No arguments are used or needed: all seem convinced that they have the truth. There is no clashing of sentiments: all are of one heart and of one mind. Our meetings are all occupied with prayer, and exhortation to love and obedience. The general expression is, "Behold the Bridegroom cometh; go ye out to meet Him."[21]

As October 22 grew near, Miller's followers made preparations for Christ's coming, not only with prayers and confession of sin, but also with the selling of their homes or farms and other earthly possessions. Those who did not sell their lands or goods left their crops untended, feeling that there was no need to work their lands or harvest their crops since Christ was returning.

They did not even think of what might occur should Christ not come.

On October 22 Millerites all over the country gathered in small groups to await the event. The day was spent in prayer, and as day stretched into evening more and more Millerites came to realize that Christ was not returning. They felt, as Miller had written before, "twice the disappointment" they had felt in the spring. On October 22 the Millerite movement crumbled.

Many turned away from the Millerite movement entirely, angrily feeling they had been duped. The leaders of the movement, Miller, Himes, and others, still expected Christ to come, maintaining again that a miscalculation had been made. A number of Miller's followers, however, stated that the 2300 days had indeed ended in 1844. They claimed that the "cleansing of the sanctuary" had indeed occurred spiritually and invisibly. These joined together into various fanatical groups. Some claimed to be sinless as a result of this invisible cleansing. Others said they were already in the kingdom of heaven on earth promised with the return of Christ, and they refused to work or support themselves. Yet another group held that the fulfillment experienced in the 1844 movement was not the Second Advent—it was yet to come. They believed, however, that the 1844 movement was a means of telling people to prepare themselves. This group decided to restudy the prophecies to see if they could discover why Christ had not returned as expected; in particular they looked again at the notion of "the cleansing of the sanctuary." "They too had accepted the popular opinion that the earth was God's sanctuary and had assumed that this 'cleansing' must refer to Christ's return to cleanse the earth by fire on the Day of Judgment."[22] Their studies led them to the conclusion that the "sanctuary" mentioned was not, in reality, the earth as they had thought, but, rather, referred to the cleansing of a *heavenly* sanctuary as described in the New Testament Book of Hebrews (Hebrews 8 and 9). The coming of Christ had yet to happen; the Advent was being prepared for.

To this group belonged the founders of the Seventh-day Adventist Church. The Millerite movement was the ground from which the Seventh-day Adventist Church grew. As did Millerites, the Seventh-day Adventist Church teaches the imminent return of Jesus Christ, but without Miller's time-setting.

The year 1844 marked the end of the Millerites as a viable movement. It also marked the start of a group and a belief that continue today. Ardent believers in Christ's return—James White, Ellen Harmon, Joseph Bates and others—came together to form the strong and lasting denomination now known as the Seventh-day Adventists. Within two months of what came to be known as "the Great Disappointment,"[23] a young girl in Portland, Maine, stepped forward saying she had had a message from the Lord that he would guide those who had trusted him in the past.

III

Ellen Gould Harmon: Her Early Years

ELLEN GOULD HARMON WAS BORN IN GORHAM, MAINE, ON November 26, 1827, four years before William Miller was to begin publicly preaching his Adventist views. In the 1800s Gorham was a small, neat town near the city of Portland. Its white houses bespoke its New England heritage.

Ellen's father, Robert Harmon, was a hatter. When Ellen was still a young child he moved his family to the city of Portland where, he felt, his business might be more successful. The Harmon family was a religious one. Ellen wrote:

> My parents, Robert and Eunice Harmon, were for many years resident of this state [of Maine]. In early life they became earnest and devoted members of the Methodist Episcopal Church. In that church they held prominent connection, and labored for the conversion of sinners. . . . During this time they had the joy of seeing their children, eight in number, all converted and gathered into the fold of Christ.[1]

As a child Ellen was a happy, sunny girl. She liked school and had hopes of continuing her education as she grew older—something few women did at that time. With her twin sister, Elizabeth, Ellen was the youngest of the eight children in the Harmon household. As was the custom in the age of home industries, the entire family helped with Robert Harmon's business. The two boys and six girls each had their parts in weaving the straw for hats, pressing the felt, or shaping the hats when finished. Life in the narrow, two-story house on Clark Street in Portland was a happy and busy one. Ellen looked forward optimistically to the future. At the age of nine, however, an event occurred that profoundly changed and influenced Ellen for the rest of her life.

Ellen and her sister, Elizabeth, attended the Brackett Street School not far from the Harmon house. One day while crossing a common with her sister and a friend, another girl, about thirteen years old, "becoming angry at some trifle, followed us, threatening to strike us," Ellen wrote when she was an adult.

> Our parents had taught us never to contend with anyone, but if we were in danger of being abused or injured, to hasten home at once. We were doing this with all speed, but the girl followed us rapidly, with a stone in her hand. I turned my head to see how far she was behind me, and as I did so, she threw the stone, and it hit me on the nose. I was stunned by the blow and fell senseless to the ground.[2]

Ellen managed to make it to her home with the help of her sister and her schoolfriend, but once there she became unconscious. She lay unconscious for three weeks. Her nose had been badly broken, and her face disfigured, so much so that her father, who had been away on business during the incident, did not recognize her upon returning home. Everyone except Ellen's mother thought she would die. A neighbor even offered, out of misplaced kindness, to buy a burial robe for her.

> When I again roused to consciousness, it seemed to me that I had been asleep. . . . As I began to gain a little strength, my curiosity was aroused by overhearing those who came to visit me say: "What a pity!" "I should not have known her," etc. I asked for a looking glass, and upon gazing into it, was shocked at the change in my appearance. Every feature of my face seemed changed.[3]

As she grew stronger Ellen felt her misfortune keenly.

> As I became able to join in play with my young friends, I was forced to learn the bitter lesson that our personal appearance often makes a difference in the treatment we receive from our companions.[4]

Ellen's twin sister, Elizabeth, was a constant reminder of how she should look. This had the effect of changing her own and others' attitudes toward herself. As if the disfigurement were not enough, Ellen faced greater disappointment when she tried to return to school. She was unable to concentrate, to learn, and she had a bad cough that further distracted her. The cough was the beginning of tubercular trouble that was with her until the age of twenty. She had to leave school for a time.

> Three years later I made another trial to obtain an education. But when I attempted to resume my studies, my health rapidly failed, and it became apparent that if I remained in school, it would be at the expense of my life. I did not attend school after I was twelve years old.[5]

Any hope of further education died for Ellen. This, with her physical disfigurement, seemed the final blow. At the age of twelve, when life is just beginning for most young people, Ellen's life seemed to have ended.

Being from a religious family, Ellen turned to prayer for consolation. During the day she helped her father with his hat-making business, at first doing only "the lightest work, that of shaping the crowns."[6] At night and in her free time she prayed and sought an understanding of what had happened to her.

Ellen wrote:

> In March, 1840, William Miller visited Portland, Maine, and gave his first course of lectures on the second coming of Christ. These Lectures produced a great sensation. And the Christian Church on Casco Street, occupied by Mr. Miller, was crowded day and night. . . . Not only was there manifested a great interest in the city, but the country people flocked in day after day, bringing their lunch baskets, and remaining from morning until the close of the evening meeting.[7]

Ellen and her family and friends attended these meetings, becoming convinced of the truth of Miller's statements. But when Miller called upon those who believed to come forward, Ellen found she could not do this. She felt she was too sinful to go forward with the other Millerites. She spoke of this to her brother, Robert, and he promised to help her by praying for her. It bothered Ellen a great deal and she spent much time thinking of it.

Later that summer Ellen's parents took her with them to a Methodist camp meeting in Buxton, Maine. Inspired by the sermon, Ellen found the courage to go forward when the believers were called. "I felt my needy, helpless condition as never before. As I knelt and prayed, suddenly my burden left me, and my heart was light."[8] Returning home to Portland, Ellen found,

> My life appeared to me in a different light. The

> affliction that had darkened my childhood seemed to have been dealt me in mercy for my good, to turn my heart away from the world and its unsatisfying pleasures, and incline it toward the enduring attractions of heaven.[9]

Soon afterward, feeling strong enough in her beliefs, Ellen was baptized into the Methodist Church. With eleven others she was immersed in the Atlantic Ocean in Casco Bay near Portland.

> Young as I was, I could see but one mode of baptism authorized by the Scriptures, and that was immersion. . . . The waves ran high and dashed upon the shore, but as I took up this heavy cross, my peace was like a river.[10]

The peace achieved by baptism did not last long for Ellen. She found it difficult to accept the idea of an angry God when she compared this idea with the joy she had felt in her own religious experiences.

> In June, 1842, Mr. Miller gave his second course of Lectures in Portland. I felt it a great privilege to attend these lectures, for I had fallen under discouragements and did not feel prepared to meet my Savior. This second course created much more excitement in the city than the first.[11]

With this second series of lectures, Ellen found some of what she had been seeking. God would forgive, Miller taught, and Jesus would return to the earth to forgive the sins of those who had prepared. Although still troubled by what she felt was her own state of sinfulness, Ellen accepted the Millerite ideas and anticipated the Second Coming of Christ. She was only one of many in Maine to do so; the strength of the Millerite movement was growing.

In 1843 the Methodist Church passed its resolution condemning the Millerite movement. It required its ministers to stop preaching Millerite ideas and stated that those members of the church who refused to conform were to leave the church. The Harmon family was among the many who were forced to leave their churches.

> The Methodist minister made us a special visit and took the occasion to inform us that our faith and Methodism could not agree . . . he stated that we had adopted a new and strange belief that the Methodist church could not accept.
>
> He advised us to quietly withdraw from the church and avoid the publicity of a trial.[12]

The Harmons insisted upon a trial within the Methodist church and there Ellen's father defended their belief in the Second Advent. But, "The next Sunday, at the commencement of the love feast, the presiding elder read off our names, seven in number, as discontinued from the church."[13]

The Harmon family continued to meet with other believers of the Millerite movement under the guidance of Elder L.F. Stockman of Portland, one of the many clergymen who, like the Harmons, had been asked to leave his church. The year 1844 was close at hand and, with it, the return of Christ according to Miller's first predictions. Prayers and preparations were fervent. At one evening prayer session, Ellen prayed so ardently she collapsed. Even with the passing of April and the failure of Miller's first prediction, the fervor did not diminish in the small group in Portland. They held fast to the belief of so many of a "tarrying time" and looked toward October, the second date Miller had set for the return of Christ. Ellen, devoted to the belief of the Second Coming, held prayer meetings with other young people and urged them to conversion.

Ellen was now sixteen years old. That summer, in 1844, a young man came to Portland to visit and speak of the expected Advent. James White, Ellen's future husband, was impressed by Ellen's piety and strength of belief, just as Ellen was moved by the young man's ardent faith in Miller's predictions. They were drawn together but, at that time, neither thought of marriage since they expected the imminent return of Christ.[14]

October 22, the day of the Great Disappointment, came and passed.

> A large class renounced their faith. Some, who had been very confident, were so deeply wounded in their pride that they felt like fleeing from the world. . . . We were disappointed but not disheartened. We resolved to submit patiently to the process of purifying that God deemed needful of us, and to wait with patient hope for the Savior to redeem his tired and faithful ones.[15]

Five weeks after the Great Disappointment Ellen Harmon was seventeen years old. Although she deeply felt the disappointment others shared, she did not give up hope. In December of 1844 her faith and hope were reconfirmed when she experienced what she felt was her first vision from God.

Ellen was visiting a friend, a Mrs. Haines, in south Portland.

> There were three other young women with them. Kneeling quietly at the family altar, they prayed together for light and guidance. As they prayed, Ellen Harmon felt the power of God come upon her as she never had felt it before. . . . Thus she entered into her first vision, in which were depicted the travels and trials of the Advent people on their way to the city of God.[16]

She experienced a renewal of hope in Adventism. October 22 had not been an end, but a beginning. Her vision, she felt, had shown her that that event was but the start of a time of preparation and would lead to the real coming of Christ. She related this vision to those with her and they, with her, rejoiced in this confirmation of their beliefs.

About a week after this event, Ellen experienced what seemed to be a second vision. In this vision God showed her that she was to be his messenger. She was shown the trials through which she was to pass and the disbelief she would meet. She was to follow her duty and relate to others what had been shown her despite these trials. This command dismayed her. How, Ellen asked, could she go out into the world, alone and frail, and achieve this enormous task? For several weeks she shrank from what she felt was her duty. She avoided both prayer meetings and her friends. Finally, she again felt urged to go out into the world. This time she could not refuse the task, the command, she felt she had been given. Still too frail to even read, Ellen Harmon set out in the bitterness of the New England winter to relate to Adventists along the coast of Maine what she had seen.

In August 23, 1915, an article in *The Independent* assessed her life:

> Did she really receive divine visions, and was she really chosen by the Holy Spirit to be embued with the charism of prophecy? . . . One's doctrine of the Bible may affect belief in her revelations. Her life was worthy of them. She showed no spiritual pride and she sought no filthy lucre. She lived a life and did the work of a worthy prophetess.[17]

When Ellen Harmon ventured out that cold winter day she set her feet upon a path that was to lead to a husband, children, and a church which, with her husband James White and others, she would help to build.

IV

Ellen Harmon, James White, and the Seventh-day Adventists

ELLEN HARMON'S MISSION WAS A DIFFICULT ONE. SHE WAS in poor health. In her travels she often met with abuse and charges of fanaticism. This was particularly so because she felt she was instructed by God to tell the people that William Miller's prophecy and the prophecies of other Adventists were false. "I was charged with being the evil servant that said: 'My Lord delayeth His coming.' "[1] The Advent would not occur until after God had tested the earth, she said. People did not believe her visionary experiences, thinking her mad or a charlatan. But Ellen persisted.

Ellen spoke with small groups of Adventists, telling her visions and urging them back to belief. She traveled through the small towns of Maine, met with people in their homes, spoke with them quietly, and led them in prayer. It was in these travels that she once again met James White and, at the age of nineteen, married him.

James White was of sturdy New England stock, his ancestors being among the earliest settlers of Maine. He was born in a small, gabled farmhouse in Palmyra, Maine, on August 4, 1821, the fifth in a family of nine children. James was a weak child because of early illness. He was unable to study regularly until he reached adolescence. At sixteen, however, his health improved and he made rapid progress in his schoolwork. At the age of nineteen he taught school while continuing his studies, and took aim at a college education.[2]

When he was fifteen, White had been baptized in the Christian church. It was not until several years later that he first heard of the teachings of William Miller. At first he held the doctrine of the Second Advent in scorn. He had returned home from his term of teaching in nearby Troy, Maine, in 1841, and found his parents seriously studying Miller's beliefs. Respecting his parents' knowledge but feeling them to be in error, he felt he should enlighten them as to the falseness of this belief. He turned to his Bible for ammunition, but found the more he studied the more he himself became convinced that what Miller said was true.

James White was of strong temperament and a determined nature. Having come to believe in the Millerite movement, he felt he should go and speak to others of it and convert them also. At the same time he also strongly desired to continue his education. Initially, his first goal of education won out and he left for Newport Academy, about four miles from his home, where he enrolled. Once there, however, he found it impossible to study. He thought more and more of the Second Coming. He began traveling to Troy to visit and pray with former students and friends. During the summer of 1842, he made his first attempts to lecture publicly on the Second Advent.

In September of that same year, William Miller, Joseph Himes, T.M. Preble, and other leaders of the Millerite movement held a camp meeting in eastern Maine. James White attended, hoping that this would help him decide whether to continue his education or follow Miller. After hearing Miller speak and studying various booklets on the Millerite beliefs, James White could no longer ignore the call within himself to go and preach. Young and penniless and uncertain of his ability to speak, he set out on what he felt was his mission.

At first his words were received with derision and disbelief, but as his ability to speak improved, he met with more and more success. He grew in repute as a speaker among Baptists, Methodists, Congregationalists, and Christians, and in the summer of 1843 he was ordained to the ministry in the Christian church.[3]

Throughout 1843 and 1844 James White preached ardently on Miller's ideas and extolled the belief of the Second Coming. The Great Disappointment was to him a personal disappointment. Had he been wrong, he questioned, and had he been misleading those he sought to teach? White thought long about this, finally coming to a conclusion similar to Ellen Harmon's that God had a greater plan, and October 22 had been but the beginning. Isaac Wellcome, a man baptized by James White (to his later regret, he said), described White as "a young man of much zeal and ambition," who "ran well for a season, though too positive on time arguments." After October 22 White got a new vision of the event and

> traveled through the country "to strengthen the little bands," as the companies were then called, confirming those who would listen, and convincing the wavering, in the idea that it was all of God.[4]

James White again met Ellen Harmon, with whom he had been so impressed in 1844. Their goals and ideas were so similar and Ellen's visions seemed to confirm them.

> August 30, 1846, "I was united in marriage to Elder James White. Elder White had enjoyed a deep experience in the advent movement, and his labors in proclaiming the truth had been blessed of God. Our hearts were united in the great work, and together we traveled and labored for the salvation of souls.[5]

James and Ellen White traveled and spoke with small groups that usually gathered in private homes.

> Our meetings were usually conducted in such a manner that both of us took part. My husband

> would give a doctrinal discourse, then I would follow with an exhortation of considerable length, melting my way into the feelings of the congregation.[6]

About this time James and Ellen White became acquainted with Joseph Bates, a retired sea captain who had been a strong leader in the Millerite movement and who continued, as did the Whites, to preach on the Second Advent. In early 1845 Bates had read an article by T. M. Preble dealing with the "Bible Sabbath," the idea of keeping the sabbath (the holy day of the week) on Saturday rather than Sunday as was traditional. Fired by this, Bates wrote a pamphlet promoting the idea. The forty-eight-page pamphlet, entitled *The Seventh-day Sabbath a Perpetual Sign*, was published in August of 1846. In meeting, both the Whites and Joseph Bates had reservations about each other. Ellen White was skeptical about Joseph Bates's stress on the seventh-day sabbath. "I did not feel its importance, and thought that Elder B.[ates] erred in dwelling upon the fourth commandment more than upon the other nine."[7]

On studying the pamphlet, however, both James and Ellen came to accept the idea of the "Bible Sabbath" and soon joined with Bates in preaching the belief. In the spring of 1847, Ellen White experienced a vision in which this belief was confirmed. Keeping the sabbath on Saturday, the seventh day as mentioned in the Bible, became an integral part of the teachings of both Bates and the Whites and part of the foundation of the Seventh-day Adventist Church.

The following years were full of traveling and speaking for the Whites. "For want of means we took the cheapest private conveyance, second-class cars, and lower-deck passage on steamers."[8] Ellen suffered from the strain of traveling, particularly while she was expecting their first child.

On August 26, 1847, the Whites' first son, Henry Nichols White, was born in Gorham, Maine, where they had settled for a time. Four children were born to James and Ellen over the years. The eldest boy, Henry, "our sweet singer," lived to the age of sixteen; the youngest boy, Herbert, died at age three months. The two middle boys, James Edson and William, lived full lives. Edson, as he was known, revealed a talent later in life as a composer and publisher of hymns. Though they were away from home a great deal, James and Ellen still provided a loving, ordered family life for their children.

The lives of the Whites, publicly and privately, centered around the now-established Seventh-day Adventist church. Both Ellen and James worked tirelessly to unify and strengthen the new church. James White served three times as president of the General Conference of the Seventh-day Adventists. The General Conference was a yearly meeting held to organize and coordinate the activities of the Seventh-day Adventist ministers and the church's many programs. Ellen White took an active hand in initiating the church's publishing, educational, and medical work, contributing not only her zeal and determination but also her writing skills.

As a child Ellen had been too ill and weak to write or concentrate. Now prayer and belief seemed to give her the strength she had lacked when she was younger. She authored a complete library during her lifetime; fifty-four books in all. Her books provided insight and guidelines on all aspects of Adventist life. Near the end of her life she wrote, "Whether or not my life is spared, my writings will constantly speak, and their work will go forward as long as time shall last."[9] Ellen's books still provide Adventists with the vision and hope they gave to early members of the church.

Organizing the small, scattered groups of Adventists was a task that took many years and met with difficulty. The Advent believers of 1844 had been cast out of their traditional churches for their beliefs, and they had developed a strong aversion to any church organization. The Whites recognized the need, however, for organization, communication, and a cohesive financial structure to support the growing community of Seventh-day Adventist ministers and their works. They and other church leaders devoted their lives to establishing these.

The Whites traveled extensively throughout the United States organizing the Adventists. Until 1855 they made their home in the eastern United States. With the establishment of the first denominational headquarters in Battle Creek, Michigan, James and Ellen moved with their children to Michigan where they lived for the next seventeen years.

On June 5, 1863, at a meeting in Otsego, Michigan, Ellen White experienced another of her visions. In it she was shown the broad principles of healthful living. Then on Christmas Day in 1865, she experienced another vision concerning the way in which to live a healthy life. These visions form the basis upon which the Seventh-day Adventists built their principles of diet and also the concepts beneath the founding of the various medical institutions they established. But these visions had in many ways a more personal meaning for Ellen White.

In 1865, James White suffered a severe stroke. After treatment in an institution in New York State, treatment which proved ineffective, they were convinced, as were other church members, that the church needed to start its own health retreat. This conviction, combined with Ellen White's visions, led to the founding of the Western Health Reform Institute in Battle Creek, Michigan, in 1866.

From 1872 until James White's death in 1881, the Whites divided their time between Michigan and the West Coast.[10] James White's death came as a great blow to Ellen. In their work and at home he had always been with her, working and sharing. She wrote

> Side by side, we had labored in the cause of Christ for thirty-six years; and we hoped that we might stand together to witness the triumphant close. But such was not the will of God. The chosen protector of my youth, the companion of my life, the sharer of my labors and afflictions, has been taken from my side, and I am left to finish my work and to fight the battle alone.[11]

James White's death was a surprise to Ellen, too, because he had overcome so much physical disability during their time together.

> Three times had he fallen under a stroke of paralysis; yet by the blessing of God, a naturally strong

constitution, and strict attention to the laws of health, he had been enabled to rally.[12]

With such perseverance, Ellen had felt he would always be with her. In August of 1881, however, after attending a camp meeting where they both caught a chill, James became very ill and died.

Alone, Ellen turned more and more to the work to which both she and James had devoted their lives. Her travels widened to include all the world. In 1885 she went to Europe and in 1891 to Australia where she helped establish Seventh-day Adventist churches. She returned to the United States in 1901 to devote her time to church work in the South and to help establish denominational headquarters in Washington, D.C., in 1903.

Although Ellen White never held church office, she was honored both within and outside the Seventh-day Adventist church as a devoted mother and tireless religious worker. The *American Biographical History of Emminent and Self-Made Men of the State of Michigan* wrote of her in 1878 that she

> is a woman of singularly well-balanced mental organization. Benevolence, spirituality, conscientiousness and ideality are the predominating traits. Her personal qualities are such as to win her the warmest friendship of all with whom she comes in contact, and to inspire them with the utmost confidence in her sincerity. . . .[13]

On July 16, 1915, this woman who was loved and

admired by a world fell asleep quietly at her home in California and died peacefully. She was buried beside her husband and children at the Oak Hill Cemetery in Battle Creek, Michigan.[14] At the time of her death, the ideas and beliefs which Ellen, with her husband James, had labored to spread were firmly established throughout the world in the Church of the Seventh-day Adventists. One fundamental belief that she personally established in the church was the belief in prophecy. As the *Seventh-day Adventist Yearbook 1987* states, "One of the gifts of the Holy Spirit is prophecy. This gift is an identifying mark of the remnant church and was manifested in the ministry of Ellen G. White. As the Lord's messenger, her writings are a continuing and authoritative source of truth which provide for the church comfort, guidance, instruction, and correction."[15] The "lighted path" of her first vision in 1844 became a highway for millions to lead them to the church she had helped to build.

V

"Sabbathkeepers" Become Seventh-day Adventists

AT FIRST THE ADVENTISTS LACKED EVEN A NAME. THE members were called the "Sabbathkeepers" or Believers in the Second Advent. Finally, on October 1, 1860, at a meeting in Battle Creek, Michigan, the name "Seventh-day Adventists" was chosen. Ellen White supported this name in opposition to other names proposed, saying, "The name Seventh-day Adventist carries the true features of our faith in front, and will convict the inquiring mind."[1] Even before the name was chosen and approved, however, the religion was being organized and was functioning.

After the Great Disappointment the organization of the Adventists was informal. It was made up of small, scattered groups of believers who would gather in a member's home to pray and talk or listen to a passing minister such as James or Ellen White or Joseph Bates. Camp meetings often were held, bringing these smaller groups together, but there was no formal organization, no formal "church."

The first formal church to recognize the Saturday sabbath was in the little village of Washington, New Hampshire. The minister of the Christian church there was Frederick Wheeler, a Methodist and Adventist minister of Hillsboro, New Hampshire, whose circuit included Washington.[2] Early in 1844 he was charged by one of his parishioners with not keeping the sabbath of the Bible—the Saturday sabbath. Wheeler went away thinking. A few weeks later, after thought and study, he kept his first sabbath on Saturday and gave a sermon explaining his reasons for doing so. This occurred in March of 1844. The seeds planted by that parishioner, Rachel Oakes Preston, were to become one of the roots of the Seventh-day Adventist church.

In that same year a more prominent preacher of the Second Advent, T.M. Preble, heard from Wheeler of this belief in keeping the sabbath on Saturday. Preble was born in New Weare, New Hampshire, and like Wheeler, traveled from church to church. In 1844, after speaking with Wheeler, Preble also began keeping and teaching of the Bible sabbath. Desiring to make this belief widespread, Preble wrote of it as well. In 1845 his first article on the subject was printed in Portland, Maine, in the Adventist periodical *The Hope of Israel.*[3]

Joseph Bates read Preble's article in *The Hope of*

Israel in March of 1845. Characteristically, he was quick to make up his mind. Here was truth. This was the way to obey the Fourth Commandment of God. This was a truth that must be spread, he felt. With the bold steps typical of Bates, he set about doing just that.

Joseph Bates was born in 1792 near New Bedford, Massachusetts, a bustling, busy ocean port that then was fast becoming the whaling center of New England. At the age of fifteen, lured by the tales of the sea he had heard while growing up in New Bedford, Bates signed on a ship as a cabin boy. His father hoped the experience at sea would make the boy want to quit, but Joseph fell in love with the sea and sailing.

While ashore in Liverpool, England, during his second voyage, Bates was impressed into the Royal Navy. It was five years before he was released. Half of that time he spent at sea and half of it as a prisoner on a man-of-war and at Dartmoor Prison in England for trying to escape from the British service.

He was finally released at the end of the War of 1812 and he returned to working on the whaling boats from America. He made ten voyages between 1815 and 1828 and was promoted from second mate and first mate to captain and part-owner of his own ship. In 1818 he married Prudence Nye, with whom he had grown up in New Bedford.[4] He fathered five children.

As Bates grew older he thought increasingly about religion. The life he had led at sea was a rough one, and he found himself thinking more and more of his life and of his sinfulness. One by one he gave up drinking, smoking tobacco, and swearing. On board his ship he initiated prayer services, a practice soon imitated by other captains. He looked for some higher purpose to his life. While still at sea, Bates wrote in his journal, "Use me O Lord . . . I beseech Thee, as an instrument of Thy service; number me among Thy peculiar people."[5]

Joseph Bates had promised his wife, Prudence, that he would retire from the sea when he had saved $10,000—an enormous amount of money at that time. In 1828 he achieved this goal and gave up his captaincy. He bought a silk farm in Massachusetts and also sold real estate. Having settled down, Bates became an active member of the local Christian Connection Church and joined several reform groups, including a temperance group and an abolitionist group.

In the early 1840s Bates heard his first Millerite sermon. He quickly became convinced of the immediacy of the Second Advent. In 1843 he left his home and set off to spread word of Miller's beliefs. He devoted both his time and money to the cause, selling his farm and real estate to support his travels and the Millerite movement. He also gave up active participation in the reform movements, saying,

> I have no less interest in temperance and in freeing of the slaves than before; but I am come face to face with a tremendous enveloping cause. When Christ comes, liquor will be forgotten and the slave will be free. The lesser causes are swallowed in the greater.[6]

The day after the Great Disappointment found Joseph Bates deeply embarrassed. He had urged his friends and neighbors to prepare for the Second Coming, and he had been wrong. Now he was taunted in the streets and called a fool.[7] Bates was nearly penniless. What he had labored for had not happened. Was all his work in vain, he wondered.

As other of Miller's followers had done, Joseph Bates turned to his Bible to study and rethink his beliefs; and like others, he came to believe his calculations were wrong. He saw what he felt was the truth in the Bible sabbath and, in 1846, after much doubt, accepted the belief that Ellen White was a true prophet. This then was to be his work: to spread the word of the Advent, the belief in the Bible sabbath, and to help organize the budding group of Sabbathkeepers.

Accustomed to travel from his experiences at sea, Joseph Bates now traveled to preach the beliefs of the Seventh-day Adventists. He sought to bring the "new light" of Adventism to people from Maine to Michigan. Joseph Bates was a rugged, determined man with the ability to hold crowds spellbound with his words. Hardship did not deter him. When he was sixty-five, one story goes, he baptized seven people in a river, standing in a hole cut through three feet of ice. The temperature was thirty degrees below zero.[8]

Bates's work took him farther and farther from his New England home and into the Midwest. He won an Adventist convert in Battle Creek, Michigan, by a simple expedient:

> Arriving in town he asked the local postmaster to name "the most honest man in town." The postmaster directed him to a traveling Merchant, David Hewitt. After Bates had expounded the Bible to him for most of a day, Hewitt was convinced, and he and his family kept the following Sabbath.

His house became the Adventist meeting place for the next three years until a church could be built.[9]

With his leadership and speaking abilities, it was natural that Bates be chosen to chair many of the meetings held by Adventists and to organize smaller groups. The Adventists at that time were, in Bates's words, "scattered sheep upon the mountains," and he diligently searched them out, organizing them together in "bands."[10] It was Joseph Bates who chaired and guided the conference of Adventists in 1860 when they finally decided to formally organize, and it was his work at this conference that influenced one of the most important meetings of the Adventists, held in Battle Creek, Michigan, in 1863. At this meeting Joseph Bates saw the culmination of all his work.

Battle Creek, Michigan, was an important town in the growth of the Seventh-day Adventist movement. In the 1860s it was a bustling town surrounded by farm communities. Ringed by green hills and situated between the Kalamazoo River and the Battle Creek, the town of Battle Creek would later become known as "The Queen City of Michigan," and was a focal point for the Adventists. It was in Battle Creek, in 1860, that the name "Seventh-day Adventist" was chosen, and, in May of 1863, it was where the various leaders of the Seventh-day Adventist groups around the country convened. Here the first Seventh-day Adventist General Conference was organized and officers elected to guide the movement. James White was nominated for president but declined because of the pressing urgency of his publishing work. John Byington was then elected president and Uriah Smith secretary. Twenty delegates attended, representing the states of New York, Ohio, Michigan, Wisconsin, Iowa, and Minnesota. At this time there were about 125 churches with an estimated membership of 3,500.

This first meeting was a jubilant gathering. For many it was the reward for years of hard work traveling and enduring hardship to spread the beliefs of the Seventh-day Adventists. Uriah Smith wrote of this conference:

> Think of everything good that has been written of every previous meeting, and apply it to this. All this would be true, and more than this. Perhaps no previous meeting that we have ever enjoyed, was characterized by such unity of feeling and harmony of sentiment.[11]

A constitution of nine articles was voted upon at this first General Conference. This served as a guide for organization of the meeting and has continued, in principle, to be a guide for General Conference meetings held since. Executive officers were elected to guide church policy during their term of office, and the General Conference was organized to have supervision of the Seventh-day Adventist work around the world. Local conferences (groups) were to direct the work in their areas, counseling and helping local churches with the supervision of the General Conference. The church itself was defined. The General Conference stated

> [A church] is composed of individual members who share the teachings of Seventh-day Adventists and are organized for worship and cooperation in carrying out the objectives of the movement.[12]

"Every member of the church has a voice in choosing the officers of the church," Ellen White later wrote.[13] The early leaders worked to make the church participatory and representative of the individual members and their beliefs.

Those beliefs, promoted by this and later General Conferences, were now confirmed. First was the belief of immortality only through Christ, which was promulgated by even the earliest pioneers of the church. They repudiated the idea of a hell for the torture of the damned, believing instead that with the return of Christ both the just and the unjust will be raised to judgment, the righteous then to receive immortality from Christ. The confirmation of this belief caused a split between some of the members of the church; some still held to the existence of a hell.

Second, the Seventh-day Adventists believed in "believer's baptism," baptism by immersion rather than just a sprinkling on of water. The third belief enunciated by the General Conference was belief in the heavenly sanctuary of God and belief that Jesus was the mediator between man and God. The fourth belief was that the doctrines of the judgment and the millennium existed. Christ would return to this earth to judge man. Fifth, the Adventists believed that because of this belief in the last judgment and the millennium, their duty was to warn the world and prepare its people for that ultimate event.

Sixth, they believed in the existence of the spirit of prophecy. They believed that this spirit was given by God to a humble human instrument for guidance in interpretation of the Bible and of Adventist conduct.

This confirmed the truth of Ellen White's prophecies for the Adventists.

Seventh, they believed in the gift of healing and of teaching the laws of health. This included founding medical programs and practicing temperance in all things. Alcohol, tobacco, tea, coffee, and meat were avoided; vegetarianism was practiced.

Last, the Adventists confirmed the belief that God meant for them to educate their children and their workers. This meant establishing schools and colleges as well as educating their children within their homes, establishing a publishing program, and organizing their churches. This latter goal was achieved by the General Conference of 1863.

Individual members and churches saw this organization as a relief from the confusion that had existed previously between Adventist groups. During the next two years, letters to the *Review and Herald*, an Adventist publication, showed the almost unanimous agreement as to the advantages of organization and the relief they experienced in finding that it worked.

With the 1863 conference the Seventh-day Adventists became an organized, mature denomination, its structure and beliefs clearly defined. Its first denominational headquarters was established in Battle Creek. All that was needed was to go and spread word of their beliefs, to send the "streams of light . . . clear round the world," as Ellen White had predicted.

VI

Early Leaders of the Seventh-day Adventists

THE MICHIGAN GENERAL CONFERENCE OF 1863 REPRESENTED many men and women who had worked long to see their ideas formally organized and who followed the church's dictates to spread belief through their publishing efforts and their educational and medical work. At first they did this without pay, supporting themselves as best they could with work of their own and by donations. But with organization came some support from the church, although at first it was very little indeed.

John Loughborough was an indefatigable worker for

the Seventh-day Adventists. A cabinetmaker in his early life, he had given up his trade to preach his beliefs, enduring the hardships, lack of support, and poverty typical of many of the early Adventist ministers. In recounting his work in New York and Pennsylvania in 1856 with ministers W.S. Ingraham and R.F. Cottrell, he recalls the first time they were given support by the church for their work:

> Funds were not furnished very abundantly for tent work, therefore during haying and harvesting, we worked in the fields four and one half days each week, for which we received $1 a day, holding tent-meetings over Sabbath and first-day of each week. In the fall, a settlement for our time with the tent was made, which was the first time that any of us had ever received a definite sum for our labor. Including what we had earned with the labor of our hands, Elder Ingraham and myself received enough to make up the sum of $4 per week, while Elder Cottrell was paid $3 per week for acting as tent-master and speaking occasionally.[1]

According to his contemporaries, Loughborough had a congenial nature and was an agreeable companion. He wrote a great deal to further the Adventist movement. His writings, while strong and serious, are filled with incidents and illustrations that provide relief from the more ponderous writings of his contemporaries. He was considered to be a pioneer evangelist for the Seventh-day Adventists and was one of the first to be paid for his services by the church. With D.T. Bourdeau, Loughborough pioneered Adventist church work on the Pacific coast and was the first official representative of the church to develop its work in England. Many times during his life Loughborough served as conference president for state conferences. He was elected as an executive officer in the first General Conference in 1863. At the end of his life, at the age of ninety-two, Loughborough was esteemed as a leader of the church. He had worked long, often in disappointment, for that honor.

In the 1850s, discouraged by poverty and at the urging of his wife, Mary, John Loughborough resigned from preaching, moved with his family to Waukon, Illinois, and returned to his trade of cabinetmaking. Shortly after he had taken this step, James and Ellen White came to Waukon to hold an Adventist meeting. They met Loughborough and urged him to accompany them on a preaching tour of the region. Loughborough agreed to go with them and, while traveling with the Whites, he had a dream that seemed related to the dissatisfaction he had felt with the Seventh-day Adventist church. So impressed was he by the dream and by the work of the Whites that

> My mind was perfectly clear in regard to my duty to go to Battle Creek and lend a helping hand in the work there. Glad am I now that I have been here to see the blessing of the Lord accompanying the arduous labors of Brother and Sister White in setting things in order.[2]

He returned to Illinois and "entered the work immediately with courage and new conviction"[3]—a conviction that was to carry him throughout the United States and across the Atlantic.

California was a rough place in the 1860s, but it was also filled with hope and opportunity for the thousands moving west. The gold rush of the 1840s and 1850s was winding down and more of those coming to California were seeking farm and ranch lands rather than gold. Food was cheap and plentiful but land—the new "gold"—was expensive.

In the 1850s a number of families holding Seventh-day Adventist beliefs followed the tide of settlers to California. They attempted to practice their beliefs and follow the church's adage by spreading the word and bringing others into the church, but they met with little success. In 1865 they sent a request to the General Conference for help in their cause, accompanying their call for help with $130 to aid with expenses.

John Loughborough and D.T. Bourdeau arrived in San Francisco on July 18, 1868.[4] They lodged with B.G. St. John, a Seventh-day Adventist of that city, and intended to hold their first tent meetings in San Francisco. When they tried to rent land, however, they found what many others were finding: the costs were too high. Discouraged, they decided against trying there but did not know where to go. Within a few days, however, it seemed their prayers for guidance were answered. A stranger called upon them and invited them, on behalf of the Independent church, to come to preach in Petaluma in Sonoma County, fifty miles north of San Francisco. Their meetings in Petaluma started them on a tour of preaching throughout the area.

While Loughborough and Bourdeau met with success in their preaching, they also ran into danger. Several times they were threatened with guns by people opposed to their views. One man said he was going to kill them because they had "lured" his daughter from him with their talk of the Second Advent. These threats caused concern in the area and members of the Adventist church came to feel that Loughborough and Bourdeau should have their own meeting place and not have to travel and confront such dangers. In the city of Santa Rosa one man donated two lots and $500 to help establish an Adventist church. Others followed with donations, resulting in the first Seventh-day Adventist church building in California. With the opening of its doors in November of 1869, work was begun in founding what is now the Pacific Union Conference, currently the largest conference of the Seventh-day Adventists in the United States.

His work in establishing the church in California well started, John Loughborough returned home to the Midwest. His days of traveling were not finished, though. In 1878 he and his wife journeyed to England to aid Adventists there in setting up their church. He recruited many followers in England despite stiff opposition from the traditional churches. He also encouraged furtherance of the work begun a few years earlier in Europe by John Nevins Andrews.

John Nevins Andrews was born in Paris, Maine, in 1829, fifteen years before the Great Disappointment of 1844. When he was seventeen years old, he and his parents accepted the Adventist views. Andrews was an editor, scholar, and writer, authoring a number of books on the Seventh-day Adventist philosophy, the best known being the monumental *History of the Sabbath*. He was to become the Adventist church's first foreign missionary when he sailed for Switzerland in 1874. Even before that, however, he displayed a missionary zeal to further the Adventist cause here in the United States.

Soon after Andrews and his parents became Adventists, the small community of believers in Andrews's hometown were subjected to the sermons of a number of fanatical preachers. These preachers had evolved strange ideas and beliefs after the Great Disappointment of 1844. They disturbed the Adventists of Paris so much that the group refused to meet, preferring to stay at home and pray rather than confront these men. When James and Ellen White came to Paris in 1849, the group of Adventists came together for the first time in a number of months.

During the meeting the Whites were interrupted by F.T. Howland, one of the fanatical preachers who had so disturbed the Adventists of Paris much earlier. Another member of the congregation drove Howland out, the others urging him on. The congregation united, it was then that Andrews uttered the statement for which he was famous in the Seventh-day Adventist church and that later was often repeated: "I would exchange a thousand errors for one truth."[5]

Andrews devoted his life to advancing what he felt was the one truth—the Seventh-day Adventist church—and to exposing what he felt was error. For example, in an article condemning O.R.L. Crosier, a man who had rejected the Adventist views, Andrews concluded: "Deeply have I regretted the course pursued by yourself, yet that the blood of souls be not found upon me, I have deemed it duty to expose it."[6]

Year by year Andrews grew in stature among the

Adventists, gaining respect for his writings and editorial work. In the autumn of 1850, the center for the publication of the various Adventist periodicals was moved to Paris, Maine. Andrews joined the publishing committee with Joseph Bates and Samuel W. Rhodes, and worked under Editor James White. Andrews became known to the Adventists because of his publication work. As a result, he was elected president at the third General Conference in 1867 and served until 1869.

In 1874 the General Conference felt the time had come to extend its missionary activities to Europe. The way had already been prepared by the publication of a Swedish Adventist paper, *Sanningens Harold*, and papers in other languages. The moment had arrived for a representative of the church itself to go abroad. The question arose as to whom to send. "Send the best," was the answer from the officers of the General Conference. John Andrews was considered the best.

When John Andrews was told of the decision of the General Conference, John Corliss wrote

> A campmeeting was appointed to convene a short distance west of Battle Creek, in the summer of 1874, just prior to the departure of our first missionary to a foreign field, and Elder Andrews was present. When the expansion of the message was dwelt upon, and notice given that he would soon leave for Europe, a change came over the meeting, and Elder Andrews, who had never appeared so solemn, at once seemed altered in appearance. His face shone with such pronounced brightness that, as I saw him and heard his apparently inspired

words of quiet contentment to be anywhere with the Lord, I thought of the story of Stephen, "whose face was as it had been the face of an angel."[7]

Andrews's wife had died in 1872. With his son, Charles, and daughter, Mary, he sailed from Boston in September of 1874, going first to England and then, in October, to Switzerland. There, with several small groups of Swiss Adventists, he held the first conference of European Adventists on November 1. The meeting set up the organization and the publication program of the Seventh-day Adventists in Europe. It also recognized the need to start work in other countries of Europe; there were few countries that had received the Adventist message. Over the next several years, Andrews traveled to Germany, Italy, France, and later, to Egypt, where he recruited and organized Adventist believers. It was in France that he found D.T. Bourdeau, who was such great help to John Loughborough. In 1876 Andrews launched the first European Seventh-day Adventist periodical, *Les Signes des Temps,* signaling the firm establishment of Adventism on continental Europe.

As Andrews worked and traveled, his health began to deteriorate and he contracted tuberculosis. His illness soon got the better of him, but even when he was confined to his bed he continued his editing and writing work. On October 21, 1883, John Andrews died in Basel, Switzerland, at the age of fifty-four, and was buried there. He died while the third conference of European Adventists was being held, with the knowledge that his work in organization and publication was well rooted and growing in Europe. His death was mourned by Adventists around the world and, later, Andrews University, in Barren Springs, Michigan, was established in his memory.

In spreading word of the Adventist beliefs through publication, Andrews had been following in the footsteps of another leader of the Seventh-day Adventists, Uriah Smith. Smith, the first secretary to the General Conference of 1863, is best known as the editor of *Review and Herald*, the church paper established by James White. Smith worked with the *Review and Herald* for fifty years and wrote numerous books and pamphlets promoting the Adventist viewpoint. His verse-by-verse commentary, *Thoughts on Daniel and the Revelation*, continues to be widely sold and read by Seventh-day Adventists.

Uriah Smith was born in West Wilton, New Hampshire. After the failure of the Millerite movement, he and his sister, Annie, came to accept the Adventist views of the Whites. Annie went with the Whites to help them with their work. Uriah wanted to pursue a career in teaching, however, and was torn between that goal and following Annie into the work of the Adventists. In September of 1852 he was persuaded to attend a meeting of Adventists at Washington, New Hampshire, where the observation of the Bible sabbath had been initiated. Visiting this church, the first church of the Seventh-day Adventists, set Smith to thinking again of his career. By December of 1852 he made up his mind to work with and for the Adventists.[8] He was joined by his sister and they both began to work for the *Review and Herald* for board and clothing only.

Uriah Smith's life was devoted to a career as a writer and editor, although he eventually was ordained as a minister. His first writing contribution to the *Review and Herald* was a long poem in blank verse, "The Warning Voice of Time and Prophecy." Throughout his fifty years with the *Review and Herald* he continued to write and edit. His work firmly established the tenor of the Adventist publishing programs.

His influence was felt in other areas also. At the first General Conference he was elected secretary, serving from 1863 until 1873 and again from 1874 to 1876. From 1876 to 1877 he filled the position of treasurer of the General Conference, and then again was reelected secretary and served from 1877 to 1881 and from 1883 to 1888. Although he held a prominent place in the General Conference, Uriah Smith was best remembered for the nearly fifty years he served as editor-in-chief of the *Review and Herald*.[9]

Uriah Smith died as he had lived, working for the Adventist cause with the *Review and Herald*. He suffered a stroke in 1903, at the age of seventy-one, while on his way to the editorial offices in Battle Creek with material ready to print.

Although Loughborough, Andrews, and Smith are only three of the many men and women who worked to form the Seventh-day Adventist church, their efforts are notable because they form the basis of two of the most important of the Adventist programs. The Seventh-day Adventist publishing and educational program and its missionary program spring from their work. Today, the programs they helped initiate are worldwide in scope.

VII

Missionary Work at Home and Abroad

THE 1860S WERE A TIME OF UPHEAVAL FOR THE UNITED States. While the Seventh-day Adventists were coming together and organizing, the United States was being pulled apart by the issue of slavery. As early as 1790 there was agitation against the slave trade by the English Quakers. Conditions under which slaves were housed and used were degrading and abusive, and the means by which they were transported from their own countries often proved fatal. One doctor, for example, who served aboard a British slave ship testified

> The slaves are so crowded below that it is impossible to walk among them without treading upon them. I was never among them for ten minutes

> together below but my shirt was wet as if dipped in water. Many are lost to suffocation in the foul air of the hold. They are closely wedged together and have not so much room as a man in his coffin, either in length or breadth. Sometimes the dead and living are found shackled together. They go down appearing to be well at night and are found dead in the morning.[1]

The slavery issue simmered for nearly one hundred years before it finally exploded into the Civil War in 1861. This war pulled the United States apart in spirit and in fact. The sympathies of the Seventh-day Adventists lay with the North and the abolitionist cause. In fact, even before the war many had taken an active part in the anti-slavery cause. Joseph Bates had been instrumental, before joining the Adventist movement, in forming an abolitionist group in his hometown of New Bedford, Massachusetts.

On January 12, 1861, Ellen White recounted a vision she reportedly had warning of a war to come.

> There is not a person in this house who has even dreamed of the trouble that is coming upon this land. People are making sport of the secession ordinance of South Carolina, but I have just been shown that a large number of States are going to join that State, and there will be a most terrible war. In this vision I have seen large armies of both sides gathered on the field of battle. I heard the booming of the cannon, and saw the dead and dying on every hand. Then I saw them rushing up engaged in hand-to-hand fighting [bayoneting one

> another]. Then I saw the field after the battle, all covered with the dead and dying . . . I was taken to the homes of those who had lost husbands, sons, or brothers in the war. I saw there distress and anguish.[2]

Like the Quakers, the Seventh-day Adventists followed the course of nonviolence. Because of this many Adventists were threatened when they refused to fight in the Civil War. During this period Ellen White wrote

> The time had come for our true sentiments in relation to slavery and the Rebellion to be made known. There was a need of moving with wisdom to turn away the suspicions excited against Sabbathkeepers.[3]

James White wrote an editorial entitled "The Nation" in the August 12, 1862, *Review and Herald* declaring the Adventists' loyalty to the northern cause. Shortly after this editorial appeared, John N. Andrews traveled to Washington, D.C., and arranged that Seventh-day Adventists be able to serve in the army in noncombatant roles.

During the Civil War the Adventists served in these positions in the army of the North, and those who were not directly involved in the war aided the abolitionist cause at home. John Byington, the first president of the General Conference, kept a station of the Underground Railroad at his farm at Buck's Bridge, New York, helping slaves escape from the South.[4]

Because of the Civil War, missionary work and the recruitment of Adventists was at first limited to the northern and western United States. Such missionary efforts as had been attempted in the South before the Civil War were interpreted by southern whites as antislavery efforts and were received with hostility.

Missionary work was, and continues to be, an important facet of the Seventh-day Adventist faith. The Adventists believe strongly in the words of Matthew: "Prepare ye the way of the Lord, make his paths straight" (Matthew 3:3), and "The gospel of the kingdom shall be preached in all the world for a witness unto all nations; and then shall the end come" (Matthew 24:14). The Seventh-day Adventists feel that each person is called to spread word of their beliefs and of the Second Coming of Christ. To facilitate this, in 1876 the General Conference called upon members to tithe as an expression of their love of Christ and to give ten percent of their incomes to support ministers and other church expenses, and to support the work of their missionaries.

During the early years of the Seventh-day Adventist church, missionary work was carried out individually. In 1853 the first preachers were sent out on an evangelical tour at the expense of the church; previously missionary work was done at the minister's own expense. The 1850s and 1860s saw the spread of the Adventist word across the northern United States. After the turmoil of the Civil War had abated, the Seventh-day Adventists turned their attention to the south and to other countries. Since work in the northern United States was firmly established, the time had come to move into places as yet untouched by the Adventists' missionary efforts. Ellen White wrote

> The light of truth for this time is now shining upon the cabinets of kings. The attention of statesmen is being called to the Bible—the statute book of the nations—and they are comparing their national laws with its statutes. As representatives for Christ we have no time to lose. Our efforts are not to be confined to a few places where the light has become so abundant that it is not appreciated. The gospel message is to be proclaimed to all nations and kindreds and tongues and peoples.[5]

Residents of the little town of Edgefield Junction, Tennessee, had received literature telling of the Adventists, their work, and their beliefs. Edgefield Junction lay just eight miles north of Nashville, south of the Mason-Dixon line. The Adventists of Edgefield Junction met together and prayed but felt they needed more guidance. In 1871 they sent a request to Battle Creek for a minister to visit them. Elbert B. Lane responded in March of that year, becoming the first Seventh-day Adventist minister to enter the South to do missionary work and recruit people to the Adventist cause.[6]

Lane looked for a place to hold meetings since there was no church in the little town. The ticket agent of the railroad offered the use of the railroad station. They were given the use of "the station and telegraph rooms . . . ," Lane reported, "The white people occupying one room and the colored the other."[7] Soon they had to use the entire station and the area around the station as, Lane continued, "My first congregations there were very small, perhaps ten or twelve, while my last were between two and three hundred."[8]

The Adventist movement spread quickly through the South after the establishment of that first church in Tennessee. Tennessee was soon followed by Kentucky in accepting Adventist views, and people in other southern states soon joined in the belief of the Second Coming. One factor slowed the church's progress in the South and created hostility between believers and non-believers: the Adventists admitted both blacks and whites to their churches. Although blacks and whites sat in separate sections of the churches, the fact that both were admitted into the same church angered many non-Adventists. During the years after the Civil War, the separation between the two races was growing wider. Racism was coming into the open.

The matter was debated in the General Conference sessions from 1877 to 1885. Most speakers held the view that Christians should not allow social questions to affect church policy. At the General Conference of 1890, however, R. M. Kilgore, who had worked in the South as a missionary, advocated the separation of white and black churches in view of the increasing hostility being shown the Adventist cause in the South. His view prevailed and led to the formal establishment of the Negro Department in the Seventh-day Adventist church in 1910 (later renamed the Regional Department in 1954), in addition to the setting up of the Southern Union Conference.

Separate churches were formed and black ministers were ordained, but still anger and threats against Adventists continued in the South. This now was due to the Adventist belief in education and in the Bible sabbath. The Adventists founded schools to educate black children and adults, an idea greeted with hostility burgeoning from the racism then rampant in the South. Both black and white Adventists also were persecuted for practicing the Bible sabbath and refusing to work on Saturdays. Many were imprisoned because of this refusal. This persecution was not confined to the South, however; many northerners also condemned the Bible sabbath. To gain understanding of their ways in such things and defend their beliefs, the Seventh-day Adventists started the periodical *The American Sentinel* in 1886, which is published today as *Liberty: A Magazine of Religious Freedom.*

Despite hostility, the South *had* opened to the Seventh-day Adventists. Adventist missionaries and workers were spreading the light, and work continued. In the 1890s and early 1900s James Edson White, the son of James and Ellen White, plied the Mississippi river in his riverboat, the *Morning Star,* which held a chapel and the printshop in which he started his *Gospel Herald,* a monthly paper telling of the gospel and of Adventists' beliefs. Later Ellen White herself visited the South to minister and encourage the educational, medical, and publishing programs there. The "light" was becoming as "abundant" in the South as it was in other parts of the United States.

The 1870s through 1890s saw the start of the Adventist church in the southern United States. Those years also marked the beginning of the foreign missionary program that led to the spread of the Adventist church throughout the world. The work available was never completed, it seemed; there was always more to do, as Ellen White wrote in 1900:

> Our watchword is to be: Onward, ever onward. The angels of God will go before us to prepare the way. Our burden for 'the regions beyond' can never be laid down until the whole earth shall be lightened with the glory of the Lord.[9]

In 1874 J.N. Andrews set out for Europe. Others were also traveling to "the regions beyond" carrying word of the Second Advent. The first Adventist churches in Canada were organized in 1877 after A.C. Bordeau and R.S. Owen held meetings in Quebec province where Joseph Bates previously had preached and prepared the way. England and Scandinavia were missionary objectives in 1878, as was Russia in 1886.

While Adventist ministers often met with hostility in their work, in Russia the first Adventist missionary minister was jailed. Early in 1886 L.R. Conradi left America to work in Germany. While there he received appeals from a Russian man, Gerhardt Perk, who, having received Adventist literature from friends, had come to follow the church's beliefs. Conradi left Basel, Switzerland, and journeyed to Russia in response to Perk's request. He had been warned by friends that no minister would be admitted to the country and so, at the border, he declared himself to be a printer.

Conradi met Perk who, enthused by his new-found Adventist beliefs, urged Conradi to travel about Russia to recruit others to the Adventist church. The two set out on a missionary journey. In Berdebulat they were both arrested and jailed for Jewish heresy—the Russians thinking that because they worshiped on Saturday they were of the Jewish faith. They also were charged for public baptism and proselytizing Russians. It took a great deal of negotiating and intervention by other Americans to at last free Conradi and Perk. Conradi left Russia almost immediately after his release. He left behind a small but growing band of Russian Seventh-day Adventists to continue his work and draw others into the Adventist church.[10]

Beginning in 1901 the European unions (the various groups of Adventists in each country) and their mission territories were treated as a unit, called at first the European General Conference and later the General European Conference. In 1903 the General Conference in the United States established a vice-president for Europe. In 1913 the European division formed its own General Conference, its officers also serving as vice-presidents of the General Conference in the United States.[11]

Up until the mid-1880s the work of the Seventh-day Adventists was concentrated in the Northern Hemisphere. In the 1880s missionary efforts turned to include the Southern Hemisphere.

> . . . first Australia, then South Africa, then the island world, then South America, then India. In the 1890s Japan was the first of the Oriental lands to hear the message. The rest of the world was to follow in the early years of the twentieth century.[12]

Adventist missionaries first entered a non-Christian continent when the General Conference sent Elders D.A. Robinson and C.L. Boyd and their wives to South Africa. They landed in Cape Town in July of 1887. Their work started among the white settlers there but missionary work among the black Africans was soon initiated. The opening of the Solusi Mission in 1894 marked the beginning of missionary work with native Africans. The Southern African Division of the church grew and developed from this start. It has since become the largest sector of the church outside North America.

The word was being spread to all ends of the earth. On October 20, 1890, the schooner *Pitcairn* left San Francisco and was soon carrying missionaries to the Pacific islands. But it was Australia, however, that came to have a rather special meaning for Adventists.

Ten years before missionaries were sent to Australia from America, Ellen White reportedly had a vision of the missionary efforts there and in other countries. She said God had shown her scenes, in various countries, where publishing houses were pouring out literature containing Adventist beliefs. When asked what countries she had seen, she replied, "The only one I can distinctly remember is Australia."[13]

On May 10, 1885, a group of Seventh-day Adventists sailed from San Francisco for Australia to carry the Adventist work to that country. The group included S.N. Haskell; J.O. Corliss and his family; M.C. Israel and his family; Henry L. Scott, a printer; and William Arnold, an experienced colporteur.[14] (A colporteur is a literature evangelist.) It was Arnold's task to precede the missionary minister around the countryside, selling books and pamphlets to prepare the people's minds for the message the evangelist minister would bring to them.

The group located their base at Melbourne. At first there was resistance to the small Adventist band. Arnold worked hard to sell books, but for the first six weeks he sold none at all. Finding churches closed against them, the group held tent meetings. Gradually, people became curious about their message. In September of 1885 the books and pamphlets Arnold had to sell began to be purchased and the Adventist message began to spread.

The group decided to start their own publishing plant instead of being dependent on literature from the United States. A little over six months after their arrival, they planned the publication of *Bible Echo* and *Signs of the Times*. The first issue was printed in January 1886.[15]

Work spread throughout the settled areas of Australia, New Zealand, and other islands. In 1891 Ellen White went to Australia and worked there for nearly ten years, helping to organize the Australasian Union in 1894, and building an educational program that would be widely emulated in other countries.

At the turn of the century, the Seventh-day Adventist church had spread around the world. It had an estimated membership of around 76,000, a membership won by the labor of the Adventist missionaries despite hazard, poverty, and hardship. The gospel of Matthew had been heeded and the "streams of light" that Ellen White had envisioned had indeed spread throughout the world. Adventist missionaries continue that work today, both in the United States and abroad, to fulfill that basic tenet of their church to spread the word and so herald the Second Coming.

VIII

"The Most Important Work": Education

EDUCATION WAS AN IMPORTANT AREA FOR THE SEVENTH-day Adventists since the beginning of their movement. As early as 1853 in Buck's Bridge, New York, and 1856 in Battle Creek, Michigan, Adventists conducted short-lived private schools to educate people both in regular subjects and in the doctrines of their church. The 1860s saw a formal start in the Seventh-day Adventist educational system.

Goodloe Harper Bell was born in Watertown, New York, and had been a student at Oberlin College in Ohio. In 1866 he traveled to Battle Creek, Michigan, to the Health Institute conducted there by the Adventists. Bell had been a public school teacher in Michigan for a number of years, but ill health had forced him to give up teaching. At the Health Institute he was given gardening and other light labor to do to build up his health. While working around the grounds of the Institute he became acquainted with a number of boys, occasionally helping them with their schoolwork. Among the boys were the two sons of the Whites, James Edson and Willie, who lived near the grounds of the Health Institute.

The boys enthusiastically told James and Ellen White of the help Bell had given them and appealed to their father to hire Mr. Bell as their teacher. James White investigated the idea, finding Goodloe Bell to be an able and talented teacher. White then hired Bell to start a school to teach the Adventist children. Bell and his family were given a building behind the *Review and Herald* printing plant on Washington Street in Battle Creek. In the upper part of the building, Bell conducted a private school. He and his family lived in the lower half of the house. In June of 1872 the first denominationally operated school opened with twelve students taught by Bell.[1] The student body quickly increased to twenty-five as word of Bell's school circulated among the Seventh-day Adventists in the area. When the fall term began, attendance was so large that the school had to move again into a new building.

The opening of Bell's school brought the question of education to the attention of the Adventist leaders. There was a need, they saw, for an educational structure within the Seventh-day Adventist church. The question was posed at large in an article in the April 1872 edition of the *Review and Herald.*

> Shall we have a denominational school, the object of which shall be, in the shortest, most thorough and practical way, to qualify young men and women, to act some part, more or less public, in the cause of God? . . . Shall there be some place provided where our young people can go to learn such branches of the sciences as they can put into immediate and practical use, and at the same time be instructed on the great themes of prophetic and other Bible truth?[2]

James White had been fortunate to find in Goodloe Bell a talented teacher who knew and wished to teach the doctrines of the Adventist church as well as traditional subjects. There were few such teachers available. It became evident that there was a need for a finishing school to train an educated clergy as well as teachers. The elementary and secondary levels of education could be carried out by the public schools for the time being. A college was needed.

The urgency of the matter was stressed in a second article in the *Review and Herald* in May of 1872

> The school must commence at the earliest point practicable. Two brethren are coming from Europe to be educated in the English language, and become more fully acquainted with our faith. . . . It is not designed to be a local affair. . . . This move-

> ment is designed for the general benefit of the cause.[3]

Ellen White gave support to this project; she had long talked of the necessity of education in the home. With the proposal of a college came an opportunity to extend Adventist teaching beyond the home and church and into church-run schools and colleges. Writing an appeal for "Proper Education" that same year (1872), she said,

> Provision should have been made in past generations for education upon a larger scale. In connection with the schools should have been agricultural and manufacturing establishments. There should also have been teachers of household labor. And a portion of the time each day should have been devoted to labor, that the physical and mental powers might be equally exercised. If the schools had been established upon the plan we have mentioned, there would not now be so many unbalanced minds.[4]

The following year, at the General Conference convening in Battle Creek on March 11, 1873, action was taken to found a school of higher education

> where "under sound moral and religious influence" men and women might be trained in the use of English and other languages spoken by the people with whom they worked.[5]

Donations to fund such a school were eagerly given.

A plot of land in Battle Creek was purchased and construction of the school building started immediately. The Battle Creek College opened in August of 1874. On January 4, 1875, when its new building was dedicated, the school had thirteen teachers and 289 students.

The school was housed in a tall, red brick Victorian building situated on a hill opposite the Health Institute in the west end of Battle Creek. The location was not in keeping with Ellen White's educational ideas. She felt the college should be located in the country, where agricultural skills could also be taught. In 1901 Ellen White strongly supported the project to move Battle Creek College into the country. That year the college was moved to Berrien Springs, Michigan, and was renamed Emmanuel Missionary College. In 1959 it became a part of Andrews University.

The interest in providing education spread among the Seventh-day Adventists. On the West Coast a small number of Adventists called for a college of their own. There was a need for educating clergy and teachers in their area also and it was too far and too expensive to send people to Battle Creek for training. Healdsburg, California, a small town in the Santa Rosa Valley, made a bid for the college. On April 11, 1882, Healdsburg College was opened. In addition to the traditional and moral education offered by Battle Creek College at that time, Healdsburg offered instruction in gardening, fruit culture, carpentry, printing, and tentmaking, courses in keeping with Ellen White's educational ideas of studying physical as well as mental skills. Healdsburg College was the forerunner of today's Pacific Union College, near Saint Helena, where it was moved in 1909.

The East Coast was not far behind the West Coast in its desire for a college. Only eight days after the opening of Healdsburg College, the South Lancaster Academy opened its doors in South Lancaster, Massachusetts. Goodloe Bell, who had been the Seventh-day Adventist's first formal teacher, traveled to Massachusetts to become the head of that college. South Lancaster eventually became the Atlantic Union College of today.

By the mid-twentieth century the Seventh-day Adventists had founded 438 colleges, academies, and schools of nursing around the world. All are directed by the Department of Education of the General Conference that was formed in 1901.

While the initial push in education by the Seventh-day Adventists was on the level of higher education, education on the elementary and secondary levels was not long in being established. At first, education in Seventh-day Adventist beliefs was taught to children at home. Ellen White's first words on education were to stress the importance of education in the home. From the Adventist ideas on home education were built the elementary and secondary church school work of the Adventists.

When Ellen White went to Australia in 1891, she immediately began work to insure the establishment of a school system.

> Wherever there are a few Sabbathkeepers, the parents should unite in providing a place for a day-school, where their children and youth can be instructed. . . . Schools should be established,

> [even] if there are no more than six children to attend.[6]

Although she had been unsuccessful in persuading the General Conference to locate Battle Creek College in the country rather than the city, she still believed that schools should be located in rural areas and teach a variety of industrial subjects. In Australia she saw a place where she could carry out her ideas of education.

> The school to be established in Australia should bring the question of industry to the front, and reveal the fact that physical labor has its place in God's plan for every man. . . . The schools established by those who teach . . . the truth for this time should bring fresh . . . incentives into all lines of practical labor.[7]

Many Australians were opposed to this idea. The majority of Australia's population was concentrated in cities; the countryside outside the cities and towns was harsh and undeveloped. Parents did not want to send their children into these rather forbidding areas. Ellen White persisted, however, and in May 1894, almost fifteen hundred acres were purchased at Cooranbang, in New South Wales, seventy-five miles north of Sidney, for a price of $4,500.[8]

The school started from the ground up. When it first was formed there were no buildings. A sawmill and tents were erected. The loft of the sawmill served as a men's dormitory and assembly hall. A school offering two classes opened on March 6, 1895, and ran for thirty weeks. The school initially enrolled only boys—and it was they who built the school. The boys went into the woods and cut down trees to build the school. The first building, a girl's dormitory named Bethel Hall, was erected late in 1896. The formal opening of the Avondale School, as it was called, came on April 28, 1897. On opening day the school had four teachers and only two students, but the student enrollment increased rapidly. One year later Avondale School had an enrollment of sixty students.[9]

Avondale School was to serve as a model for later schools of higher grades in the Adventist educational structure. It incorporated all the ideas on education that Ellen White had previously advocated but had not been incorporated in the college founded at Battle Creek. Avondale proved the soundness of those ideas and led to their incorporation when later schools were established by the Seventh-day Adventists.

While Ellen White was working in Australia to organize the Adventist educational program there, education was making similar progress in the United States. In the spring of 1897, E. A. Sutherland, president of Battle Creek College, received a request from a farmer living near Bear Lake, Michigan, named Albert Alkire. Alkire wrote to ask if the college might send an Adventist teacher to teach his five children. Until that time there were no Adventist elementary schools that were not part of the teacher-training Adventist colleges.

Alkire was only one of a number of Adventists who wished to have their children taught in Adventist schools. While Sutherland was attempting to provide a teacher for Bear Lake, other requests for teachers arrived at the college. On the first of November, 1897, he called for volunteers from among the advanced students and many responded. Five schools were established within two or three weeks of one another, in late November and early December of 1897. Before a year had gone by there were fifteen such schools.[10] This was the beginning of the movement in elementary and secondary education of the Adventists, a movement that has grown rapidly over the years. Today the Seventh-day Adventists maintain the third largest parochial school system in the United States.

There was a substantial amount of opposition among the Adventists to establishing the elementary school system. Many felt that this would be an unnecessary expense to Adventists since the public schools were available. Others objected that it would take funds from the work of the church and its foreign missions, which they felt were more important. The supporters of the educational program prevailed, however, their cause strengthened when Ellen White wrote in favor of the idea from Australia.

The early Adventist teachers had little to work with. There were no school buildings at first; classes were usually held in one room of a church member's home. All teachers in the beginning years were paid fifteen dollars a month and board. There were no blackboards or other equipment with which to teach. Early teachers had to "make do."

In many ways those early teachers were extreme in their ideas of teaching. Often, as much of their own education had been in the instruction of the Bible, they made the Bible the only textbook in their schools, using it to teach not only reading but also arithmetic, geography, and physiology. This was in spite of the fact that

Seventh-day Adventist educators had long before prepared schoolbooks on grammar and geography, and the colleges were hurrying to prepare readers and arithmetic books. It was a number of years before a standard curriculum was established by the church and teachers instructed to use texts other than the Bible.

The Bible was not disgarded completely. It was and continues to be the source of instruction in Adventist schools. Ellen White wrote

> True education means more than the preparation for the life that is now. . . . It is the harmonious development of the physical, the mental, and the spiritual powers. It prepares the student for the joy of service in this world, and for the higher joy of wider service in the world to come.[11]

The stress of Adventist education is to train children and young people for Adventist work as educators, missionaries, doctors, nurses, or other occupations that help others and to spread the word of the Seventh-day Adventist beliefs.

> All the natural sciences are to be studied in the light of God; all the social sciences are to be illumined with the purpose of God; all the mathematical sciences are to be seen as an expression of God's mind. "The Bible" is to be "made the foundation and the life of all study."[12]

The textbooks and instruction in Seventh-day Adventist schools center on the premise that the Bible provides a guide for viewing all areas of study. Things not of the Bible are not studied. Darwinian evolution, the theory that man is descended from primates, is not taught in Adventist schools, and is a concept strongly denied by Seventh-day Adventists. Adventist writer Arthur W. Spalding wrote

> Is there room for the study of science? Yes, most emphatically. But not for the study of science apart from the Maker of science. Not for a science that knows not God but man, a science that starts with doubt and ends in conjecture.[13]

Adventists believe that the creation of the world and of man is that set down in the Bible, not that proposed by Darwin or any other man. The origin of man is told in the Bible, hence Darwin's theory of evolution is not taught in Seventh-day Adventist schools and colleges.

Most of the schools founded by the Adventists followed the example of the Avondale School to a lesser degree and set up programs dealing with agriculture and other areas of manual education. Domestic sciences are also studied in the schools, with diet and health key points of instruction. Seventh-day Adventists believe in and are taught the virtues of vegetarianism, abstinence from tobacco, alcohol, and other stimulants such as tea and coffee. Modesty in dress is urged; showiness in clothing and the wearing of jewelry is discouraged.

The Seventh-day Adventist educational system begins in the home. Parents are instructed by the Adventist church to begin teaching their children early, believing in the words of Solomon: "Train up a child in the way he should go: and when he is old, he will not depart from it" (Proverbs 22:6). At an early age children are taught stories from the Bible and are told stories and read books about the Adventist life and movement.

This system of education, beginning in the home and extending through higher education, assures the Seventh-day Adventist church of a continual supply of missionary-minded men and women to carry Adventist beliefs throughout the world. By 1980 the Seventh-day Adventist church had 3850 elementary schools, 800 secondary schools, 1 correspondence school, 79 colleges, and 3 universities.[14]

Ellen White wrote in 1903 that "True education means more than the pursual of a certain course of study. It means more than a preparation for the life that now is. It has to do with the whole being, and with the whole period of existence possible to man. It is the harmonious development of the physical, the mental, and the spiritual powers. It prepares the student for the joy of service in this world, and for the higher joy of wider service in the world to come. . . ."[15] Education was a means of fulfillment, in all respects.

IX

Healing Hands: Medical Missionary Work

THE PRINCIPLES OF HEALTH AND DIET TAUGHT IN THE Seventh-day Adventist schools have been emphasized since the founding of the Adventist faith. This emphasis developed into a cause and has made the prevention and treatment of disease a major goal of the church.

Joseph Bates had crusaded for temperance and "wholesome food" from the time he joined the Adventist movement. Even before he accepted the Adventist views, he gave up alcohol, tobacco, coffee, and tea and adopted vegetarianism. He urged others to join him; and some did, but many pioneers of the movement were oblivious to his message. Their thoughts and activities were taken up with proclaiming the message of the Adventists. They saw nothing wrong with eating meat or having a cup of tea.

In 1848 James and Ellen White joined Bates in his drive against tobacco, tea, and coffee. In 1851 Ellen White wrote, "Those who use tobacco, tea and coffee should lay aside those idols, and put their cost into the treasury of the Lord."[1] By 1853 the *Review and Herald*, the official publication of the Adventists, contained numerous articles supporting this view. In 1855 the sentiment had grown so strong that the Vermont Conference voted that those members who were tobacco users must leave their congregations.

Temperance in alcohol was never an issue in the Seventh-day Adventist church as most members of the church had joined the temperance crusade early. The reforms in diet urged by Joseph Bates, however, were the basis for many arguments. Gradually more and more members of the church came to see his side of the issue. John N. Andrews wrote in 1871:

> I did not know that late suppers and "hearty" ones at that were serious evils. I had no idea of any special transgression in eating between meals; and though this was mostly confined to fruit, I did herein ignorantly trangress to a very considerable extent. I supposed old cheese was good to aid digestion! Do not smile at my folly; unless my memory is at fault, I had learned this out of "standard medical works". . . . In less than five years I was utterly prostrated.[2]

Andrews resisted the health and diet reforms of Joseph Bates and the Whites. He came to believe in them, as his writing indicates, after he suffered a breakdown in his health. He was not alone in his resistance; a good many other Seventh-day Adventists also scoffed at the ideas.

Ellen White had been concerned with health and diet all her life. Both she and her husband had been sick when they were children and their health as adults still was not good. In 1863 she began counseling members of the Seventh-day Adventist church to adopt more healthful practices. In 1865 Ellen White wrote:

> In the vision given me in Rochester, New York, December 25, 1865, I was shown that our Sabbathkeeping people have been negligent in acting upon the light which God has given in regard to the health reform, that there is yet a great work before us, and that as a people we have been too backward to follow in God's opening providence as He has chosen to lead us.

One way in which she felt she was directed to promote health reform was by opening a place where people could come when they were ill.

> Our people should have an institution of their own, under their own control, for the benefit of the diseased and suffering among us who wish to have health and strength. . . . Such an institution, rightly conducted, would be the means of bringing

> our views before many whom it would be impossible for us to reach by the common course of advocating the truth.[3]

At the General Conference of 1866, church leaders resolved to establish a health institution in keeping with Ellen White's principles. She had urged again, at the conference, that, "We should provide a home for the afflicted and those who wish to learn how to take care of their bodies that they may prevent sickness."[4] Such an institution would not only treat disease but also teach the ideas of temperance and vegetarianism and be a means to reach people and spread Adventist ideas. The ministers at the General Conference responded favorably and pledged themselves to adopt what Ellen White felt were the correct habits of life. They also voted to carry on the work of education in health as a part of their ministries, and voted to found a health institution as one means to carry these convictions into action.

Although the financial situation of the Seventh-day Adventists was poor, the Civil War having strained the people's pocketbooks, they worked hard to bring about the creation of a health institution. A large piece of property and a house were obtained in Battle Creek, Michigan. By September of 1866 the Western Health Reform Institute opened its doors. Dr. Horatio S. Lay, who had earlier treated James White during an illness, was chosen to head the institute. Lay also started a journal entitled *The Health Reformer* that advocated the Adventist ideas of health. It was issued in August of 1866, shortly before the institute opened. Its name was later changed to *Good Health* and since has been succeeded by a number of other health journals, the best known in America today being *Life and Health*, published at Adventist headquarters in Takoma Park, Washington, D.C.

The health institute opened with

> two doctors, two bath attendants, one nurse (untrained), three or four helpers, one patient, any amount of inconveniences, and a great deal of faith in the future of the Institution and the principles on which it was founded.[5]

Despite the inconveniences and limited equipment it initially had, the institute appealed to many and soon one patient had grown to be many patients. The institute regime included health and diet reform and discouraged drug therapy. Patients were urged to do light work and to be ambulatory rather than bedridden.

During the early 1870s concern was felt among the Adventists that the Health Institute was losing sight of its goals and becoming merely a fashionable sort of spa. The Institute was overcrowded and many church members urged that larger buildings be erected. James and Ellen White, however, with other church officials, saw that the problem was that there were not enough physicians to adequately handle the number of patients. In the fall of 1872 they sent four young people to the Hygieo-Therapeutic College in New Jersey for training as physicians. "At the end of the course James White encouraged the most promising of the four, John Harvey Kellogg . . . to attend the Medical School of the University of Michigan and then loaned him $1,000 for further education at Bellevue Hospital Medical College in New

York."[6] In 1875 John Harvey Kellogg joined the staff of the Institute and in 1876 he was appointed medical superintendent. Kellogg was soon involved, not only in the administration of the Health Institute, but also in issuing health literature and in the education of young people in the medical and nursing professions. Under his leadership, the Institute quickly returned to its original goals.

Kellogg was an ardent worker in the fields of health and medical care, and also in exploring and promoting his religious beliefs. Under his directorship the Institute erected in 1878 a new building on the grounds of the original Institute with the approval of the Whites and other church members. In 1877, James White had said, "Now that we have men of ability, refinement, and sterling sense, educated at the best medical schools on the continent, we are ready to build."[7] In the same year, the Institute was renamed the Battle Creek Medical and Surgical Sanitarium. During its first decade, from 1866 to 1876, the Institute had served two thousand patients, of which ten had died, an unusually low number in those days.[8]

John Harvey Kellogg was an unusual man and an indefatigable promoter of better health through "biological living," encouraging vegetarianism, proper exercise and the avoidance of tobacco, alcohol and other stimulants. He lectured to groups across the nation on his principles and published nearly fifty books on his views. He condemned the practice of women wearing corsets because it prevented them from breathing naturally. He is best remembered, however, among the general public for his development of a flaked cereal, a development which began the flaked breakfast cereal industry in America; his brother, W. K. Kellogg, made it an international industry.[9] Among his other inventions are a vibrating chair to increase the circulation of the blood, a vibrating belt to similarly aid circulation and to help in weight reduction (this has since become a standard piece of equipment in weight-reducing salons), and the universal dynamometer, a strength-testing device.

While Kellogg was building his own reputation and that of the sanitarium, he was, at the same time, losing the favor of Ellen White and the Seventh-day Adventist leaders. In 1902 the sanitarium burned to the ground. With Kellogg's urgings, plans were drawn for a new structure which was to be magnificent in size and in decoration. On May 1, 1902, Ellen White wrote to him: "Last night I was instructed to tell you that the great display you are making in Battle Creek is not after God's order. You are planning to build in Battle Creek a larger sanitarium than should be erected there."[10] Despite Ellen White's protests and those of other church leaders, the new, "extravagant" sanitarium was dedicated the following year.

Kellogg was also losing the Adventists' favor because of his views. He had begun as a Seventh-day Adventist, but his naturally inquiring mind had led him to the exploration of the nature of his religious beliefs. He began to promote a kind of pantheism, the belief that God is an essence pervading all nature. This was in direct conflict with Adventist beliefs, and a leader of the church counseled him to stop these speculations. Ellen White wrote him numerous letters, privately warning Kellogg to halt this line of study. Kellogg persisted, though, and in 1903 privately printed, although forbidden to do so by the Seventh-day Adventists, a book entitled *The Living Temple* in which he explained his views.

The publication of *The Living Temple* brought to a head the conflict between John Kellogg and the Seventh-day Adventists. Ellen White, who had long defended Kellogg, was forced to condemn the book publically.

> Pantheistic theories are not sustained by the word of God. The light of His truth shows that those theories are soul-destroying agencies. . . . These theories, followed to their logical conclusion, sweep away the whole Christian economy. They do away with the necessity for the atonement, and make man his own savior.[11]

The Living Temple and the controversy that followed its publication led to a break between Kellogg and the Seventh-day Adventists. Many of those who had worked with Kellogg followed him in his move away from Adventist beliefs. This led, in 1907, to the withdrawal of Adventist support and control of the Battle Creek Sanitarium, which continued under the directorship of Kellogg. Although it no longer exists today, the Battle Creek Sanitarium was the forerunner of the 239 Adventist hospitals and clinics that now exist around the world.

A significant outgrowth of the work done at the Battle Creek Sanitarium stemmed directly from Dr. Kellogg's program of medical and nursing education. In 1884 a two-year nursing course was started. Nursing courses were to become a feature of all the large sanitariums and hospitals established by the Seventh-day Adventists. In the early 1890s this training program at Battle Creek was strengthened by the establishment of the Medical Missionary Nurses' Training School, which was restricted to those who wanted to devote their lives to the missionary side of medical work.[12]

The need for trained physicians who practiced Adventist medical reforms was also becoming acute. Too often the physicians hired by the sanitarium did not hold with the Seventh-day Adventist beliefs in diet reform or avoidance of drug therapy. The Seventh-day Adventists realized the necessity of training their own physicians. In 1895 the American Medical Missionary College opened in Chicago under the guidance of John Kellogg. The College lasted fifteen years but went out of denominational control along with the Battle Creek Sanitarium in 1907.

In 1909 Ellen White spoke to the General Conference of the need for medical missionaries.

> There are souls in many places who have not yet heard the message. Henceforth medical missionary work is to be carried forward with an earnestness with which it has never yet been carried. This work is the door through which the truth is to find entrance to the large cities, and sanitariums are to be established in many places. . . . Our sanitariums are to be schools in which instruction shall be given in medical missionary lines.[13]

That same year, heeding that call, the College of Medical Evangelists was established in Southern California.

The College of Medical Evangelists began with two

divisions. One was formed at Loma Linda to train nurses and dietitians and provide classwork for the first two years of the medical course. A second school in Los Angeles offered the advanced courses of the medical college. The two are now united at Loma Linda, as the medical school of Loma Linda University, established in 1961.

The college at Loma Linda had previously been known as the College of Loma Linda Evangelists. In 1905 Elder J. A. Burden located a resort hotel for sale near San Bernardino, California. It seemed the ideal location to start a school and sanitarium, and with the encouragement of Ellen White, Burden set about raising the necessary funds. Within six months he managed to raise the down payment and the college was soon organized. Today, Loma Linda University is the largest of all the Seventh-day Adventists' educational institutions.

The emphasis of Seventh-day Adventist medical training is on its missionary aspects; it is considered one more way by which the word of Adventism can be spread. As Ellen White wrote

> As unbelievers shall resort to an institution devoted to the successful treatment of disease and conducted by Sabbathkeeping physicians, they will be brought directly under the influence of the truth. By becoming acquainted with our people and our real faith, their prejudice will be overcome and they will be favorably impressed. . . .
>
> Some who go away restored, or greatly benefited, will be the means of introducing our faith in new places and raising the standard of truth where

> it would have been impossible to gain access had not prejudice been first removed from minds by a tarry among our people for the object of gaining health.[14]

With that view in mind, medical missionary clinics and sanitariums have been founded all over the world, some in the remotest regions, to bring both health and Adventist beliefs to others. The work by these missionaries has been arduous and often accompanied by deprivation, but it has not been without recognition both from Seventh-day Adventists and non-Adventists. Dr. Stanley G. Sturges, a 1955 graduate of Loma Linda University, was chosen one of "America's Ten Outstanding Young Men of 1961" by the United States Junior Chamber of Commerce for his work in Nepal. Sturges typifies the efforts of many of the Adventist medical missionaries since the beginning of that work.

X

Work for All

"THIS WILL BE THE MOST IMPORTANT CONFERENCE EVER held by the Seventh-day Adventist people," conference president George A. Irwin said at the opening of the 1901 General Conference in Battle Creek.[1] He spoke before 237 delegates from around the world representing a membership then estimated at about 76,000.[2] The conference was gathered to debate and vote upon a very controversial issue, that of reorganization of the Seventh-day Adventist administration. Adventists feared the results.

The Adventist church had grown to such an extent since 1863 that the leaders felt that the time had come to reorganize to ensure everyone a voice in the church. There was criticism that the sole authority for the church lay with a small group of men: the General Conference executive officers. Greater representation of the members of the church was needed, many felt, to reduce the authority of that small governing group and encourage greater freedom of action and enterprise.

Over the years a number of independent associations had evolved from the work of various Adventists. The church leaders worried that because these associations, such as the International Sabbath School Association, were not directly under church control, they might deviate from Adventist goals. Church leaders felt there was a need to bring these groups under the shelter of the church and, at the same time, distribute the responsibility for these groups to those who were doing the actual work within them.

The Committee on Reorganization presented numerous suggestions at the General Conference. The final voting resulted in the following organization.

1. The world was organized into "union conferences" and "union missions." This meant that several local conferences within a territory made up a union. The union directed those conferences with approval from the General Conference. This distributed some of the administrative responsibility instead of having direction come solely from the General Conference. There were to be eight union conferences in North America; five union conferences in Europe, making up the General European Union Conference; and the Australasian Union Conference. Union missions consisted of areas where Adventist work was undeveloped or just beginning. The union missions were placed under the supervision of the General Conference.

2. The General Conference was to be run by a committee of twenty-five people who represented all areas

of Adventist work. This committee since has been enlarged as the church and its work has grown.

3. Various independent organizations of an Adventist nature, such as the International Medical Missionary and Benevolent Association, were given representation on the General Conference. The governing bodies of these independent groups were, in turn, to be composed of people drawn from their own memberships and also drawn from the General Conference. This insured closer ties between the General Conference and these organizations.

4. Union conferences were to be self-governing and self-supporting. Where possible, however, they were under the injunction to tithe, to support the Seventh-day Adventist church as a whole, and to devote their efforts to spreading Adventist beliefs throughout the world.

The Seventh-day Adventist church became more representative of its individual members. Ellen White wrote

> The church chooses the officers of the state [or local] conferences. Delegates chosen by the State conferences choose the officers of the Union Conferences; and delegates chosen by the Union conferences choose the officers of the General Conference. By this arrangement every conference, every institution, every church, and every individual either directly or through representatives, has a voice in the election of the men who bear the chief responsibilities of the General Conference.[3]

Leaders of the Adventist church had viewed the General Conference of 1901 with trepidation. They feared chaos would come from the efforts to reorganize, that dissension would emerge between different interests and cause a split within the church. The reorganization had just the opposite effect, however; it created a new era of unity, reform, and financial solvency for the Seventh-day Adventists.

Change seems to beget change and with the reorganization of the church administration came new perspectives on other issues. One of these was the moving of the headquarters of the church away from Battle Creek. In December of 1902, ten months after the Battle Creek Sanitarium had burned, the plant of the Review and Herald Publishing Association in Battle Creek also was destroyed by fire. Many, including Ellen White, felt this was a sign that the General Conference headquarters and the publishing headquarters should be relocated. Just as the General Conference of 1901 had redistributed responsibility, the burning seemed a call to redistribute the resources of the church and reach out to other areas and people the Adventists had not yet touched. The Atlantic seaboard was seen as a good place from which to focus these efforts. Ellen White spoke in favor of this move at the 1903 General Conference.

> Let the General Conference offices and the publishing work be moved from Battle Creek. I know not where the place will be, whether on the Atlantic Coast or elsewhere. But this I will say, Never lay a stone or brick in Battle Creek to rebuild the Review Office there. God has a better place for it. He wants you to work with a different influence,

> and [to be] connected with altogether different associations from what you have had of late in Battle Creek.[4]

Battle Creek was too isolated from the rest of the world that the Seventh-day Adventists wished to reach. In addition, it had unpleasant memories for many leaders of the church because of the dispute with John Kellogg. Although quite a few were opposed to such a move, the majority were for relocation, and a place was sought.

In the midsummer of 1903, the decision was reached to relocate to Washington, D.C. Being on the Atlantic coast allowed the Seventh-day Adventists access to the world for missionary purposes and also access to the government so that Seventh-day Adventist interests could be promoted when necessary. A tract of land was purchased for church headquarters in Takoma Park, about six miles from the center of the city. An estate of about fifty acres in Maryland also was obtained on which to build a college and sanitarium.

> These were the beginnings of the present institutions at headquarters: the General Conference, the Review and Herald, the Washington Sanitarium, and Washington Missionary College.[5]

The area was very rural when the first buildings were erected by the Adventists. Since that time the city of Washington, D.C., has expanded to surround the Adventist headquarters.

The new century had brought to the Adventists a new cohesiveness and had provided for expansion in new directions. The reorganization and the move to Washington, D.C., enabled the leaders of the church to give more attention to work in the field, both at home and overseas, and to the various groups that carried out that work in the field. There was work for all Adventists to do to spread their beliefs. One of the most important groups working with this goal in mind was the colporteurs.

In 1870 a young Canadian, George King, came to Michigan with a desire to enter the ministry. After working with other ministers and then being given a chance to preach, it was decided by his superiors that he was not talented at preaching. Because he wanted to work for the Seventh-day Adventists in some way, he was given the job of selling pamphlets and books about the Adventist movement. George King was so successful in this task that by 1881 he was training other colporteurs. The General Conference eventually took the work of the colporteurs formally under its control.

The task of the colporteur, or literature evangelist, is to bring people the gospel message in printed form by visiting from home to home. A secondary goal is, of course, to raise money for the Adventist church through the sale of these books and pamphlets. Supplying the colporteur today are forty-two Adventist publishing houses located around the world. The colporteurs are drawn from the lay members of the church. They originally worked in conjunction with the International Tract and Missionary Society, now the Publishing Department, formed in 1874 by Stephen N. Haskell. The colporteur sells books by subscription and thereby supports a body of volunteer workers.

During the 1890s and early 1900s, there was a decline in colporteur work in America. America was experiencing a financial depression during the 1890s. Money was scarce, and people did not buy the books sold by the colporteur. Many colporteurs were forced to turn to other work to support themselves.

With the reorganization of the General Conference in 1901, the distressed book work came under the scrutiny of the committee. A concentrated effort was proposed to enlist members of the church as colporteurs. To aid in providing material for them to sell, the Publishing Department of the General Conference was formed from the International Tract and Missionary Society. The Publishing Department was appointed to oversee the efforts of the three main publishing companies of the Seventh-day Adventists in the United States, although leaving their separate corporations intact. The three were the Review and Herald Publishing Association in the East; the Pacific Press in the West; and the Southern Publishing Association in the South (as of 1901). By arrangement with these publishers, the colporteurs would be provided, at special rates, with material to sell.

Arthur G. Daniells, president of the General Conference from 1901 to 1922, called upon conference presidents, schools, and church members, urging the promotion of colporteur work. "I believe we are now standing on the verge of a great revival of the canvassing and missionary spirit," he told students of Battle Creek College in 1901. "I pray that the students who are here will join us and be among the very first to take hold of this work."[6]

The result of Daniells' campaign was a resurgence of colporteur work—work considered by Ellen White and other church leaders to be the most important work that could be done by the lay members of the church. Daniells' efforts also led to the establishment of the student colporteur plan. By an arrangement between the schools and the publishing houses (with both providing partial financial support), students can sell books and accumulate commissions equal to a year's scholarship at the Adventist school of their choice during their vacation or any time of the year.

While the student colporteur plan helps young people gain an education, there are many other programs for young people in the church to help them with everyday life and prepare them for adult roles in the church. Concern for children and young people was evident from the start of the Adventist movement. One of James White's early editorial ventures (1852) was *Youth's Instructor,* a magazine intended for both children and young people. The reorganization in 1901 also took into consideration the young people of the church. In 1901 work with the youth of the church was organized in connection with the Sabbath School Society and put upon a formal footing.[7]

Groups of young Adventists had formed sporadically over the years. There was no formal organization for young people until the turn of the century. In 1907 a convention held at Mt. Vernon, Virginia, proposed the formation of the "Seventh-day Adventist Young People's Society of Missionary Volunteers." The General Conference soon after approved the Young People's Missionary Voluntary Department and encouraged a program to organize Junior Missionary Volunteer Societies in churches and Adventist schools.

A meeting of the Educational and Missionary Volunteer Council held at St. Helena, California, in 1915 felt there was a need for greater structure in the various Junior Missionary Volunteer (JMV) Societies. The societies were to stress "the harmonious development of the physical, the mental, and the spiritual powers" of the young Adventists. This led to the formation of JMV courses with different levels of achievement. Friend, Companion, Explorer, and Pioneer classes were established for the junior members; Guide and Master Guide classes for senior members. The objective of the JMV and the Young People's Department is "To Save from Sin and Guide in Service" young people of the church. The work of the JMV is three-fold: educational, social, and missionary. Their aim is "The Advent Message to All the World in This Generation."[8]

Classes for the JMV are held in Adventist churches, schools, and summer camps. They teach youth about the history of the church; its goals; its views on dress, health, and diet reforms; and train young Adventists for local missionary work.

Other groups for young people also came from the work of the Young People's Department. Two such groups are the Pathfinders, an organization similar to the Boy Scouts, and the Medical Cadet Corps.

The Medical Cadet Corps was developed in 1939 and placed under the guidance of the National Service Commission of the Seventh-day Adventist church. In 1954 it was renamed the National Service Organization. In 1939 war was raging in Europe and all indications were that the United States would not be able to avoid involvement in the war. Adventists have always believed in nonviolence. The church leaders felt there was a need to prepare their young men to assume noncombatant positions in the military should the United States enter the war.

The Medical Cadet Corps trained young men in basic military drill, medical and technical subjects such as those they might be assigned in the military, and the Adventist principles of noncombatancy. The latter was to help the young men understand the reasons behind the church's stand on noncombatancy and to enable these young men to explain it to others who otherwise might not understand their position. Members of the Medical Cadet Corps served bravely in World War II. After the bombing of Pearl Harbor, many distinguished themselves by acts of heroism in helping to save their fellow soldiers.

After World War II the Medical Cadet Corp and its activities declined. It was revived and strengthened in the United States and other countries in 1950. Today, in addition to its original purposes, the Medical Cadet Corps also works to prepare young men interested in entering the medical profession.

The Seventh-day Adventist church calls upon all its members, young and old, male and female, to further its work through various missionary activities. These activities range from professional work as a medical missionary, teacher, colporteur, or minister, to the informal work of JMV members speaking of Adventist beliefs to non-Adventist friends and others. Since the 1901 reorganization church members are active in all levels and phases of church operation. Adventists feel there is a job for each member within the church and work for all in spreading the Adventist movement.

XI

New Ways to Spread "Streams of Light"

EARLY ADVENTIST MINISTERS PREACHED WHEREVER THERE was an audience that would listen. They were often untrained and unpaid, but they were inspired and made converts wherever they went. The first theological schools of the Seventh-day Adventists were the home study courses, Sabbath schools, and tent and camp meetings. The teachers were parents, church leaders, colporteurs, and evangelistic preachers. If a young man decided to become a minister, he often was taken on as a sort of apprentice by an already established evangelist minister. The young man would assume the role of "tent master." It was his job to erect, strike, transport, and store the tent used by the minister at tent meetings. He also cared for the grounds around the tent, advertized the meetings by putting up posters, bought provisions, and led the singing. Under the guidance of the evangelist minister, the young man was to study at every opportunity and, at last, try his skill at preaching. If he was successful, after a time he would be ordained and assume a ministry of his own.

This was an arduous and haphazard method of training, and it soon became evident to church leaders that a more formal, organized type of training was needed. In 1874, when Battle Creek College was founded, it was primarily a theological school to train ministers. "The chief subjects of study were the law of God, with the instruction given to Moses, sacred history, sacred music, and poetry."[1] This training was thought to adequately prepare young men to assume the duties of a minister; further study was left to the individual to do on his own. Many ministers, however, felt they could use help in continuing their studies.

In 1920 in Australia a group called the Ministerial Association was formed. They began the Ministerial Reading Course and published a journal, *The Evangelist,* to facilitate the exchange of information among Adventist ministers. The aim of both the reading course and *The Evangelist* was to aid Australian ministers in their independent studies.

The General Conference of 1922 took note of the work in Australia and voted to form a general organization similar to the Australian group to help all Adventist ministers. Arthur G. Daniells was elected secretary of the newly formed Ministerial Association in the

United States. In 1928 the Association expanded to cover the various unions around the world.

At first the Ministerial Association issued a monthly mimeographed newsletter for the exchange of information. In 1927 this was succeeded by the journal, *Ministry.* In addition, the Ministerial Reading Course, started in 1914 by the Department of Education of the General Conference, was taken over by the Ministerial Association. *Ministry* not only allows an exchange of Adventist views but also presents articles, letters, and comments by non-Adventist clergy to help both Adventist and non-Adventist clergy keep current with events and opinions in the religious world in general.

The Ministerial Association grew over the years in response to the needs of the Seventh-day Adventist ministers. Its duties are to gather material that would be helpful to ministers and Bible instructors, to act as a clearinghouse for suggestions, and to give special attention to young men who are studying for the ministry.

Although the Ministerial Association was helpful in furthering the education of ministers, it soon became evident that formal post-graduate training of the church's clergy and teachers needed to be offered to increase their effectiveness in carrying the Adventist message. A first step toward this was taken in 1933 when the Autumn Council of the General Conference voted to form the Advanced Bible School to be held in summer sessions at various Adventist colleges. These were short courses to help Adventist clergy with advanced study. The Advanced Bible School sessions were instituted the following summer, in 1934, and proved so popular among the ministry that church leaders felt thought should be given to forming a regular program of postgraduate studies.

In 1936 the Autumn Council changed the name of the Advanced Bible School to the Seventh-day Adventist Theological Seminary and voted to begin construction of a permanent school that would run year round. The site chosen was on the land adjoining the General Conference headquarters and the Review and Herald building at Takoma Park. The seminary was dedicated on January 21, 1941.

From its beginning the Theological Seminary stressed the spiritual and practical aspects of ministerial work. The faculty was composed of clergy who taught the scholarly side of study, and others with field experience to train students in missionary work. It offered a Master of Arts, a Master of Arts in Religion, and Bachelor of Divinity degree. In 1959 the Theological Seminary was moved to Berrien Springs, Michigan, where it now forms one of the graduate divisions of Andrews University.

In addition to reaching people directly by training for the ministry and preaching, the Seventh-day Adventists have attempted to reach others through various media and communications technology as it developed. At the start of the Adventist movement, the only medium available was the printed word. In 1848 Ellen White told her husband, James, that she had a message for him:

> You must begin to print a little paper and send it out to the people. Let it be small at first; but as the people read, they will send you means with which to print, and it will be a success from the first.

> From this small beginning it was shown to me to be like streams of light that went clear around the world.[2]

The Adventists had previously published books and pamphlets but no journals, papers, or magazines. In 1849 James White began to publish the *Present Truth*. In 1888 Ellen White wrote,

> My husband then began to publish a small sheet at Middletown, eight miles from Rocky Hill [Connecticut], and often walked this distance and back again, although he was then lame. When he brought the first number from the printing office, we all bowed around it, asking the Lord, with humble hearts and many tears, to let His blessing rest upon the feeble efforts of His servant. He [James White] then directed the paper to all he thought would read it, and carried it to the post office in a carpetbag.[3]

The following year, in 1850, *The Advent Review* began publication and soon merged with the *Present Truth* to become the *Second Advent Review and Sabbath Herald* (the *Review and Herald*). This semimonthly became a weekly in 1853 and continues to the present as the *Adventist Review*. The publishing offices of this paper were first established in Rochester, New York, and, in 1855, moved to Battle Creek, Michigan, where denominational headquarters were then located. Following a fire in its building in 1902, the *Review and Herald* was moved to Takoma Park, Washington, D.C., and then to Hagerstown, Maryland, where it is still located. The *Adventist Review* remains the foremost publication of the Seventh-day Adventists, although it is now supplemented by numerous other publications dealing with specific concerns or groups within the Seventh-day Adventist Church. As of June 1986, the church published 89 different general periodicals in English alone; around the world it publishes a similar number of periodicals in 74 different languages.[4]

In 1912 a new convert to Adventism, who was also a newspaperman, Walter L. Burgan, pointed out the need for public relations within the Adventist church. Under his direction the Bureau of Press Relations was formed. The bureau contains a staff of reporters and writers to cover the larger meetings of the church. It maintains cordial relations with the national press, sending out press notices; it has a clipping service, and alerts church agencies to movements, trends and events of interest to the church. By the end of the second decade of the twentieth century, the Seventh-day Adventist publishing program was firmly established around the world as a rapidly developing means to publicize events within the church.

As new technology developed the Adventists used the new media to carry their message. By 1930 the radio was commonplace in the average American home. "If only I could preach on the radio," evangelist H.M.S. Richards of Los Angeles said, "I could reach thousands of people with the gospel where now I am reaching only hundreds." Richards prayed for the funds to broadcast an Adventist radio program. While preaching one night he asked his audience to donate old jewelry to buy time on the radio. They responded with enthusiasm, and soon the *Tabernacle of the Air* program was a regular radio show. At first this was just a fifteen-minute devotional program, but as the program grew in popularity it was expanded to include preaching and music.

In 1937 Glenn A. Calkins, president of the Pacific Union Conference, became interested in what Richards was doing. Under Calkins' guidance the program was promoted to various interests and sponsors and reorganized to become *Voice of Prophecy*. With Richards preaching and the King's Quartet providing music, *Voice of Prophecy* reached an eighteen-state audience.

The success of *Voice of Prophecy* was noticed by the General Conference. At its Autumn Council in 1941, it was voted to make nationwide use of the radio to proclaim the Adventist message. The Radio Commission was formed by the General Conference, and on January 4, 1942, *Voice of Prophecy* broadcasts became nationwide over eighty-nine stations.[5]

Within a month of the first nationwide *Voice of Prophecy* program, the church also started broadcasting the *Bible School of the Air*, a Bible correspondence school introduced by F.W. Detamore. During the first month more than two thousand listeners enrolled in the course, and soon it expanded to include the blind in its correspondence course. A Junior Bible Correspondence course was instituted a few months later. By the middle of the twentieth century, enrollment in the courses was estimated at around 35,000.

Radio broadcasts in other countries and languages quickly followed those in the United States. In 1948 the Radio Commission, which by then had grown to include a North American and an international branch, was dissolved and reformed as the Radio Department of the General Conference. Its function was to oversee and promote national and local Adventist radio broadcasts both in the United States and other countries.

With the start of television, the Radio Department was renamed the Radio-Television Department in 1956. The Seventh-day Adventists were quick to see the advantages of television in spreading their message. The first television programs, as with the first radio programs, were local, produced by individual ministers and their congregations. In 1950 Pastor William Fagal began broadcasting *Faith for Today* on a local station in New York City. The first program of *Faith for Today* was shown in May 1950. It grew in viewer popularity, and by the end of the year, it was being shown by approximately ten stations on the ABC network. By the end of 1965, it was being shown by 265 stations here in the United States and by stations in Korea, Trinidad, Brazil and Nigeria. Since then it has expanded to include most countries in the world.[6]

Pastor Fagal and his wife conducted half-hour programs of five different types:

> (1) the "parable" type (dramatic sketches relating the Bible to everyday life situations, combined with a sermonet); (2) interviews with missionaries; (3) mission travelogues; (4) sermon documentaries; and (5) all-music programs.[7]

This popular format is still used today in the current *Faith for Today* television broadcasts. The Faith for Today Headquarters is in New York City. The program is now the oldest denominationally-sponsored television program today.

In 1971 the Adventist World Radio was started in Europe and the Adventist Media Center was established in Thousand Oaks, California. At present, in addition to the *Faith for Today* television program, the Seventh-day Adventist church also produces two other television shows. *It Is Written* is in its thirty-first year of broadcasting and is shown on 130 stations in North America, Australia and the Caribbean. *Breath of Life* is the church's newest television program, designed especially for black audiences. It has been seen in many metropolitan areas of the United States, Bermuda and the West Indies.

In the Bible (Revelation 14:6–12) God's final message to the world is symbolized by three angels carrying messages of the world. Ellen White wrote that "The influence of these messages has been deepening and widening, setting in motion the springs of action in thousands of hearts, bringing into existence institutions of learning, publishing houses, and health institutions."[8] She foresaw the widening influence of the Seventh-day Adventist church through its publications and its schools and hospitals. Today the Adventist message is also spread through the use of the sophisticated technology of radio and television.

XII

Loma Linda: A Ministry of Healing

WITHIN THE LAST TEN YEARS, THE NON-ADVENTIST "MAN on the street" hears of the Seventh-day Adventist movement most frequently in an indirect manner through the announcements of the medical developments being made at Loma Linda University Medical Center. The man on the street is probably not even aware that Loma Linda is an Adventist educational and medical institution, yet his life and all our lives are affected positively by the efforts being made there, efforts that are an extension of earlier Seventh-day Adventist principles.

In 1902 Ellen White predicted that "unoccupied properties" in California would become available at far below their actual value. She urged that these be purchased for the purpose of establishing sanitariums.

> In various places, properties are to be purchased to be used for sanitarium purposes. Our people should be looking for opportunities to purchase properties away from the cities, on which are buildings already erected and orchards already in bearing. Land is a valuable possession. Connected with our sanitariums there should be lands, small portions of which can be used for the homes of the helpers and others who are receiving a training for medical missionary work.[1]

Two such properties were found almost immediately and were purchased; they are, today, the Paradise Valley Hospital and the Glendale Adventist Medical Center.

But Ellen White wished for a school to be established to train medical missionaries also, and in 1904, John Burden, the manager of the St. Helena Sanitarium near San Francisco, found a property between San Bernardino, Riverside, and Redlands that matched a description given to him by Ellen White. It was the land and buildings of a resort called Loma Linda ("Hill Beautiful").

The facilities had originally been built as a resort community in the 1880s, then sold to a group of physicians who had planned to turn it into a health resort. The group of physicians had put a great deal of money into Loma Linda but it had not been successful and they were desperate to sell. After some negotiating they finally agreed to sell the property, estimated at

$155,000 in value, at the unheard of price of $40,000. Even at that price John Burden hesitated for he knew that he did not have the money. He consulted Ellen White and she urged him to obtain the property. She said, "Move forward in faith, and money will come from unexpected sources."[2] Surprisingly, through unanticipated donations the money did become available and the Loma Linda property was purchased.

> The principal building was a large frame structure of sixty-four rooms, the sanitarium; there were four large cottages, a large recreation hall, a pumping plant furnishing abundant water, and pleasant grounds; and there were seventy-six acres of land surrounding and enclosing the hill, eighteen acres of it in orange and grapefruit groves."[3]

In November of 1905 the Loma Linda Sanitarium and School of Nursing opened.

Ellen White had stressed that Loma Linda was to be "not only a sanitarium, but also an educational center," and on September 20, 1906, the Loma Linda College of Evangelists opened. Initially the college offered four courses: collegiate, nurses, gospel workers, and a three-year evangelistic-medical course.[4] When the college opened that September, there were no students, but by October, thirty-five students had enrolled and by 1909 it was time, the administrators felt, to formally make it a medical school. The name was changed to the College of Medical Evangelists and in December of 1909 a charter was obtained from the State of California authorizing it to grant degrees in the liberal arts and sciences, dentistry and medicine. It initially received a "C" rating from the American Medical Association, but as the years passed and new facilities were added—in 1913 a division was opened in Los Angeles for the clinical training of doctors—that rating rose. Loma Linda University received its "A" rating on November 16, 1922.[5]

Throughout the last years of her life, Ellen White energetically supported the developing medical school and urged other Adventist leaders to do so also. It was important, she felt, that the college provide the best training available and graduate the best doctors and nurses possible. "The medical school at Loma Linda," she said, "is to be of the highest order. . . . Whatever subjects are required as essential in the [medical] schools conducted by those not of our faith, we are to supply."[6]

The College of Medical Evangelists became Loma Linda University in 1961 and has continued to pursue that goal of excellence established by Ellen White so long ago, achieving it again and again in many areas of training and research. Today Loma Linda University is the educational heart of the worldwide Seventh-day Adventist healthcare service.

Just as the Adventists were quick to recognize the advantages of the new technologies of radio and television to spread their message, so too, in the area of medical research, have they been quick to utilize the advantages of computers and developments in technology. "The Scientific Computation Facility (SCF) at Loma Linda University Medical Center has developed computer programs that help the physician in more rapid and accurate diagnosis of a variety of medical problems."[7] By using computers Loma Linda University Medical Center researchers have developed programs that produce electrocardiograms and vectorcardiograms for the research and treatment of heart disease. "The vectorcardiogram shows the path of the heart's electrical impulse looping through the computer heart model *in three dimensions* . . . thus giving the physician a top, front, and side view of the loop. He can then compare abnormal loops with normal."[8]

Many techniques of medicine have been researched and developed at Loma Linda by its doctors and graduates, greatly adding to the knowledge and treatment of a variety of conditions. Much of the pioneer work on fetal monitoring, for example, was done at Loma Linda by Edward H. Hon, M.D. (Class of 1950). He started his research on fetal monitoring while on the faculty of Yale University in 1955, utilizing his extensive background in electrical engineering. This work was continued at Loma Linda during 1960–1964 and again at Yale "where in 1969 he developed the world's first fetal intensive care unit."[9] Fetal monitoring has become almost commonplace today, but its impact was significant. A 1969 report in *Life* magazine pointed out that, until Dr. Hon's research, "Some five to seven infants per thousand die unexpectedly each year. . . .

"Hopefully, Mr. Hon's new system could save as many as 20,000 babies a year."[10]

A second significant medical technique developed at Loma Linda University Medical Center has been the "Loma Linda University Technique" of dental pain control by Professor Niels Bjorn Jorgensen D.D.S. who taught in the School of Dentistry from 1954 to 1974.[11] This utilizes a controlled intravenous drip for sedation rather than general anesthesia. The technique reduces anxiety and pain for a patient and, because the patient is awake, it maintains a patient's cough reflex and allows him to cooperate with the dentist. In addition, because the patient is relaxed, he is capable of opening his mouth wider.

The Judkins Technique of Transfemoral Selective Coronary Arteriography, introduced in 1966 and developed by Melvin P. Judkins, M.D. (Class of 1947), is yet another contribution to medicine by Loma Linda University Medical Center.[12] It is now the world's most widely used technique for the X-ray evaluation of blood vessels of the heart and is used in determining the necessity of such operations as coronary bypasses.

Although it had achieved a reputation within the medical community for its advances in medicine, Loma Linda University Medical Center did not reach national attention until the 1980s when its baby heart-transplant program was initiated. On November 20, 1985, Dr. Bailey and his surgical team performed the first successful heart transplant on a four-month-old baby. At that time no successful transplant had been done on a child so young. Since then Dr. Bailey and his team have performed transplants on eleven more babies; most recently, in October of 1987, a transplant was performed on a baby who was only three hours old.

The success rate of the baby heart-transplant program at Loma Linda is exceptional. Of the eleven babies who have undergone this radical surgery, eight have survived. This is a phenomenal rate of survival compared to the survival rate of other medical centers that are doing similar operations.[13]

The baby heart-transplant program at Loma Linda University Medical Center has, from necessity, led to the development of many new techniques. One such advance has been in testing for levels of cyclosporine in the blood. Cyclosporine is an immuno-suppressive drug used in transplants. The former test took about eight hours. Because the transplant team was working with babies, who react to medication and other changes more rapidly than adults, it was necessary to develop a test that did not take so long. Researchers at Loma Linda developed a technique for testing that is more accurate than the older technique, less expensive—and takes only one hour.[14]

One of the greatest undertakings at Loma Linda University Medical Center is under construction, a proton beam accelerator for the treatment of cancer. Developed by the Loma Linda University Medical Center in association with the Department of Energy's Fermi National Accelerator Laboratory in Illinois, the accelerator, called a synchrotron, consists of one fixed beam and three isocentric rotating gantries three stories high using approximately 250 million volts of power.[15]

The advantage of using protons in the treatment of cancer over traditional radiation is that protons can be controlled; the therapy can actually increase the radiation dosage to a tumor while *reducing* any dosage to surrounding, healthy tissues. "The continuously variable energy of the proton beam allows flexibility in varying the depth of radiation penetration. Thus, radiation energy can enter the body at a very low absorption rate, and then increase sharply at a specific point, called the Bragg Peak . . . with little or no radiation on exit."[16]

The synchrotron will be unique in four respects: (1) it will be the first accelerator in the world designed and built for a hospital setting; (2) it will be the only accel-

rooms, and; (4) it will be the only accelerator with isocentric *rotating* gantries so that the beam can be focused with precise accuracy.[17]

The developments at the Loma Linda University Medical Center are exciting to everyone but in particular for Adventists; they are a sign of fulfillment of Ellen White's desire that "The medical school at Loma Linda is to be of the highest order." But Loma Linda University Medical Center is more than just a center for research, it is also a hospital, a place where caring counts. The Adventist staff of the medical center feel that their jobs are not only ministering to the physical needs of a patient but also to his mental, emotional, social and spiritual needs. This is in keeping with the Adventist ideas of spreading their message. Ellen White wrote:

> As unbelievers shall resort to an institution devoted to the successful treatment of disease and conducted by Sabbath Keeping physicians, they will be brought directly under the influence of the truth. By becoming acquainted with our people and our real faith, their prejudice will be overcome and they will be favorably impressed. . . .
>
> Some who will go away restored, or greatly benefited, will be the means of introducing our faith in new places and raising the standard of truth where it would have been impossible to gain access had not prejudice been first removed from

> minds by a tarry among our people for the object of gaining health.[18]

Loma Linda University Medical Center is a place of healing but it is also a ministry in which the Adventists' message can be heard and spread throughout the world.

XIII

The Messages of the Three Angels

FROM THE EARLY DAYS OF THE SEVENTH-DAY ADVENTIST movement, with a traveling minister holding small meetings in a home or a tent, to the televised programs of today reaching millions, the Adventist church's goal has been to spread the message of "the three angels" mentioned in the Bible (Revelation 14:6–12). The first angel's message is an announcement that the Day of Judgment is come. The Seventh-day Adventists preach that this means that the time has come to give up the artificial life of the world and turn to the study of God and the Bible.

The second angel's message of "Fallen, fallen is Babylon the great, she who has made all nations drink the fierce wine of her fornication!" (Revelation 14:8) is, for the Seventh-day Adventists, a call to leave decadent and corrupt organizations. It is an injunction to study the truth and avoid apostasy in the churches.

The third message (Revelation 14:9–12) is a call to direct special attention to God's commandments and the faith of Jesus. This message is of special importance to the Seventh-day Adventists as, for them, it means that they are to devote their lives and their work to God.

The Seventh-day Adventist church has been devoted to carrying out the instructions contained, they feel, in the messages of the three angels in Revelation and in the messages given to them by Ellen White. From the time they are children and are taught by their parents, through college, a member of the Seventh-day Adventist church studies God and the Bible. They give up the "artificial life" by shunning jewelry and extravagant clothing, and by practicing the rules of diet and health laid down by Ellen White, Joseph Bates and other early leaders of the church. The lives and work of the Seventh-day Adventists are devoted to God through the missionary work done by all to spread the Adventist message. Adventists work to bring the message that the Second Coming of Christ is anticipated, by publishing, through medical missionary work, teaching, television, or simply by talking with others.

In 1844 Ellen White reported that she was called by God to travel and, "I was shown the trials through which I must pass, and that it was my duty to go and relate to others what God had revealed to me."[1] Setting out that winter, she could little anticipate that the small band of believers who would first join her would expand to include the thousands who still follow her words today. She hoped, and that hope was confirmed, that the message she had to bring to others would be the basis of the church which now encircles the world.

The Seventh-day Adventist church started with a few people and grew to include many and continues to grow today. As of June 1986, the number of baptized church members was 4,863,047 with 26,135 organized churches and 10,490 ordained, active ministers. As of 1984 the church was working in 184 countries around the world.[2] As a Christian church, the Seventh-day Adventist church is small. However, it is one of the fastest growing churches in the world—seven percent growth a year.[3]

The Seventh-day Adventists today are unique among organized religions in that, since inception, the church has been representative of its members, each church constituency electing its own officers. The overall organization of the Seventh-day Adventist church today reflects this representative nature. At the base is the local church governed by elected officers: elders, deacons, deaconesses, clerks, treasurers and department leaders. In essence, the local church is a microcosm of the church as a whole. The minister to a church is appointed by the local conference.

The local conference is made up of all the local churches in a specific area, and is responsible for all church and evangelistic work in that area. Officers of the local conference are elected every three years by delegates from member churches.

The next level of organization is the union conference which consists of several local conferences in a specific area and which operates all church colleges and universities in its area as well as directing the local conferences. Officers and directors of a union conference are elected every five years. As of 1986, there were 84 unions within the Seventh-day Adventist church, representing 410 local conferences, missions and fields.

A division is comprised of two or more union conferences covering a large area. Officers and departmental directors are elected at a general session of world delegates held every five years. There are ten divisions within the Seventh-day Adventist church.

The General Conference, of which the divisions are a part, is the head of the Seventh-day Adventist church. Officers and directors of the General Conference are elected every five years at the general session.[4] The territory of the General Conference is "The land area of the world. . . ,"[5] and its departments include: the Church Ministries Department (organized in 1985); Communication (established in 1972); Education (1902); Health and Temperance (reorganized in 1980); the Ministerial Association (organized in 1922); Public Affairs and Religious Liberty (organized in 1902); and Publishing (organized in 1902). The General Conference also oversees a number of other services, corporations, institutions and organizations.[6]

Ellen White wrote that "Many families who, for the purpose of educating their children, move to places where our large schools are established, would do better service for the Master by remaining where they are. They should encourage the church of which they are members to establish a church school where the children within their borders could receive an all-round, practical Christian education." "We are far behind our duty in this important matter. In many places schools should have been in operation years ago."[7]

Ellen White and other early Adventist leaders felt that, in order to best follow Adventist ways, schools should be established for all ages. Those desires have been amply fulfilled today. In 1986 there were 5,458 schools operated by the Seventh-day Adventist church and 52,609 Sabbath schools.[8] The Adventist child has an opportunity to learn of his or her church not only by attending Sabbath school but also by attending one of the 4,306 primary and elementary schools, one of the 914 secondary schools, or one of the 94 colleges and universities operated by the church. Institutions of education exist for every age child and adult so that they need not be exposed to the beliefs and manners of nonSabbathkeepers, need not be corrupted by the ways of the world. "God has called His church in this day," wrote Ellen White, "as He called ancient Israel, to stand as a light in the earth. By the mighty cleaver of truth, the messages of the first, second, and third angels, He has separated them from the churches and from the world to bring them into a sacred nearness to Himself."[9]

Although there is a separation between Seventh-day Adventists and the world, that separation is not complete; to be so would be to violate the interpretation of the three angels' message that it is necessary to spread the word of Adventist beliefs throughout the world. As was mentioned previously, the message is spread by deed, in the Seventh-day Adventists' medical programs, and by word, through publication and through the media. In 1986 there were 152 Seventh-day Adventist hospitals and sanitariums, and 292 dispensaries, clinics and launches throughout the world ministering to the needs of both Adventists and nonAdventists.[10]

In addition to helping those who are ill, the Seventh-day Adventists try to guide the well to the road of healthier living. The Seventh-day Adventists run a number of stop-smoking clinics and also manufacture health-food products. The church operates twenty-eight food companies for this purpose.

In the field of publication, the Seventh-day Adventists have come a great distance from the publication of one small eight-page periodical, the *Present Truth*, published in 1849 by James White. The Adventist church now operates fifty-one publishing houses throughout the world, producing literature about the church in 189 languages.[11] There are approximately 6,829 literature evangelists or colporteurs distributing that literature, as well as numerous book centers through which the literature is sold. The Adventist message, indeed, is spread to the ends of the earth.

For the Seventh-day Adventists the work of repentance and reform is an integral part of faith, especially at the present time. For many Adventists, the 1980s are a time of special trial. "Something is happening to the delicate machinery we call civilization. It still operates, but deep in the gears we hear strange sounds, as if the machine itself were breaking up."[12] The question many Adventists are asking is how to survive during what appears to be a coming period of chaos. The answer, for them, lies in the fundamentals of the Seventh-day church as set down by Ellen White and others: eschew cities and establish oneself in rural areas; eat naturally; exercise; live simply. One Adventist book, *How to Survive the 80's*, suggests just such things, techniques thought of by Ellen White more than one hundred years ago. The Seventh-day Adventists seek to survive the corruption of the world and its concomitant chaos in order to, at last, see the "new earth," the earth cleansed by the millennium.

> On the new earth, in which righteousness dwells, God will provide an eternal home for the redeemed and a perfect environment for everlasting life, love, joy, and learning in His presence. For here God Himself will dwell with His people, and suffering and death will have passed away. The great controversy [regarding the character of God, His law, and His sovereignty over the universe] will be ended, and sin will be no more. All things, animate and inanimate, will declare that God is love; and He shall reign forever.[13]

Significant Dates in Seventh-Day Adventist History

1755 November 1, Lisbon, Spain. One of the most severe earthquakes on record occurred.

1780 May 19. The "Great Dark Day" in which darkness lasted for approximately fifteen hours starting between 10 and 11 A.M.

1782 William Miller born in Low Hampton, New York.

1792 Joseph Bates born near New Bedford, Massachusetts.

1821 James White born in Palmyra, Maine.

1827 Ellen Gould Harmon (White) born in Gorham, Maine.

1833 November 13. The "Falling of Stars," a large meteor shower is seen over the United States.

1844 The Great Disappointment.

The first Sabbathkeeping Adventist group formed in Washington, New Hampshire (later organized as a Seventh-day Adventist church in 1862).

1849 First paper published by the Seventh-day Adventists, the *Present Truth,* printed in Middletown, Connecticut.

1850 First issue of the *Second Advent Review and Sabbath Herald* (the *Review and Herald,* now called the *Adventist Review*) printed in Paris, Maine.

1852 *Youth's Instructor* first published.

1853 First preachers sent out on an evangelistic tour at the expense of the Seventh-day Adventist church.

1855 *Review and Herald* office moved to Battle Creek, Michigan.

1860 The name, Seventh-day Adventist, adopted by the church on October 1.

1863 General Conference of the Seventh-day Adventists organized and constitution adopted.

1866 The Western Health Reform Institute (later called the Battle Creek Sanitarium) opened to patients.

The first health journal, *Health Reformer*, published.

1868 John Loughborough and D. T. Bourdeau arrive in California to begin missionary work resulting in the formation of the Pacific Union Conference.

1871 First denominational college opened (Battle Creek College, later Emmanuel Missionary College, then re-formed as Andrews University).

The first missionary, J. N. Andrews, sent overseas to Switzerland.

1881 James White dies at Battle Creek, Michigan.

1884 First denominational training school for nurses formed at the Battle Creek Sanitarium.

1885 Missionary work begun in Australia.

1889 National Religious Liberty Association formed (later changed to the International Religious Liberty Association).

1897 Formal dedication of the Avondale School in Australia on April 28.

1898 Southern Missionary Society incorporated.

1901 Reorganization of the General Conference administration.

Organization of the departments in the General Conference begun.

Young people's work organized in connection with the Sabbath School Department.

1903 General Conference headquarters and the Review and Herald Publishing Association moved to Washington, D.C.

1907 Church withdraws support from the Battle Creek Sanitarium.

Young People's Missionary Voluntary Department formed.

1909 College of Medical Evangelists established in southern California (later Loma Linda University).

1912 Press Bureau (now the Bureau of Public Relations) formed.

1913 General Conference organized into divisions.

1915 Ellen White died July 16 at St. Helena, California.

1922 Ministerial Association organized.

1927 *Ministry* first published.

1934 Advanced Bible School organized and given in summer sessions at various colleges.

1939 Medical Cadet Corps organized.

1941 Theological Seminary at Takoma Park dedicated on January 21, 1941.

Radio Department of the General Conference organized.

1942 *Voice of Prophecy* first broadcast on a coast to coast radio network.

Bible School of the Air introduced to radio.

1950 *Faith for Today* first broadcast as a network television show.

1955 Seventh-day Adventist membership reaches above the one million mark.

1956 First university established in Washington, D.C. (reorganized as Andrews University in 1960 at Berrien Springs, Michigan).

1961 Loma Linda University organized (opened in 1962).

1971 Adventist World Radio started in Europe.

Adventist media center established in Thousand Oaks, California.

1983 *Review* and *Herald* printing plant moved to Maryland.

1985 First baby heart transplant performed at Loma Linda University Medical Center.

1986 Seventh-day Adventist membership reaches nearly five million.

1988 Construction started on a proton accelerator at Loma Linda University Medical Center.

Notes

Chapter 1

[1]Falkner, Leonard For *Jefferson and Liberty: The United States in War and Peace, 1800–1815* (Alfred A. Knopf: New York, 1972) p. 3.

[2]*Ibid*, p. 4.

[3]Miller, Douglas T. *Then Was the Future: The North in the Age of Jackson, 1815–1850* (Alfred A. Knopf: New York, 1973) p. 2.

[4]*Ibid*, p. 4.

[5]Cable, Mary, and the editors of *American Heritage American Manners and Morals* (American Heritage Publishing Co.: New York, 1969) p. 97.

[6]Miller, p. 20.

[7]Cable, p. 89.

[8]*Ibid*, p. 98.

[9]*Ibid*.

[10]Katz, William L. *Eyewitness: The Negro In American History* (Pitman Publishing Corp.: New York, 1968) p. 102.

[11]Cable, p. 89.

Chapter 2

[1]White, Ellen G. *Testimonies for the Church*, Vol. I (Pacific Press: Mountain View, CA, 1948) p. 21.

[2]Maxwell, C. Mervyn *Tell It To The World* (Pacific Press: Mountain View, CA, 1977) p. 9.

[3]*Ibid*, p. 11.

[4]Sellers, Charles & Henry May *A Synopsis of American History* (Rand McNally & Co.: Chicago, 1963) p. 103.

[5]Maxwell, p. 11.

[6]Cooper, Emma Howell *The Great Advent Movement* (Review & Herald Publishing Assn.: Washington, D.C., 1968) p. 13.

[7]Maxwell, p. 13.

[8]Spalding, Arthur *Origin and History of Seventh-day Adventists*, Vol. I (Review & Herald Publishing Assn.: Washington, D.C., 1961) p. 19.

[9]Cooper, p. 13–14.

[10]Maxwell, p. 16.

[11]*The Telescope* Bond Astronomical Club: Cambridge, MA, October 1934.

[12]Devens, R.M. *Our First Century* (C.A. Nichols & Co.: Springfield, MA, 1876) p. 329–330.

[13]Devens, p. 330.

[14]Schaefer, Richard A. *Legacy* (Pacific Press: Mountain View, CA, 1978) p. 28.

[15]Cooper, p. 15.

[16]*Ibid*, p. 31.

[17]Spalding, p. 88.

[18]Cooper, p. 32.

[19]Spalding, p. 53.

[20]*Ibid*, p. 94.

[21]*Ibid*, p. 94–95.

[22]Schaefer, p. 35.

[23]Cooper, p. 35.

Chapter 3

[1]White, Ellen G. *Testimonies for the Church*, Vol. I (Pacific Press: Mountain View, CA, 1948) p. 9.

[2] *Ibid.*
[3] *Ibid*, p. 10.
[4] *Ibid*, p. 11.
[5] *Ibid*, p. 13.
[6] Spalding, Arthur W. *Origin and History of Seventh-day Adventists*, Vol. I (Review & Herald Publishing Assn.: Washington, D.C., 1961) p. 61.
[7] White, p. 14.
[8] *Ibid*, p. 17.
[9] *Ibid*, p. 19.
[10] Ibid, p. 19–20.
[11] Ibid, p. 21.
[12] Ibid, p. 41–42.
[13] Ibid, p. 42.
[14] Spalding, p. 69.
[15] White, p. 56.
[16] Spalding, p. 71.
[17] Utt, Richard *A Century of Miracles* (Pacific Press: Mountain View, CA, 1963) p. 15.

Chapter 4
[1] White, Ellen G. *Testimonies for the Church*, Vol. I (Pacific Press: Mountain View, CA, 1948) p. 72.
[2] Spalding, Arthur W. *Origin and History of Seventh-day Adventists*, Vol. I (Review & Herald Publishing Assn.: Washington, D.C., 1961) p. 45.
[3] *Ibid*, p. 51.
[4] *Ibid*, p. 54–55.
[5] White, p. 75.
[6] *Ibid.*
[7] *Ibid*, p. 76.
[8] *Ibid*, p. 77.
[9] White, Ellen G. *Testimony Treasures*, Vol. 1 (Pacific Press: Mountain View, CA, 1949) p. 16.
[10] *Ibid*, p. 15.

[11] *Testimonies for the Church*, Vol. I, p. 105–106.
[12] *Ibid*, p. 105.
[13] *Testimony Treasures*, Vol. 1, p. 18.
[14] *Ibid*, p. 17.
[15] *Seventh-day Adventist Yearbook, 1987* (Review & Herald Publishing Assn.: Hagerstown, MD, 1987) p. 7.

Chapter 5

[1] Spalding, Arthur W. *Origin and History of Seventh-day Adventists*, Vol. I (Review & Herald Publishing Assn.: Washington, D.C., 1961) p. 303.
[2] *Ibid*, p. 115.
[3] *Ibid*, p. 118.
[4] Maxwell, C. Mervyn *Tell It To the World* (Pacific Press: Mountain View, CA, 1977) p. 76–77.
[5] *Ibid*, p. 78.
[6] Spalding, p. 29.
[7] Maxwell, p. 79.
[8] *Ibid*, p. 80.
[9] Utt, Richard *A Century of Miracles* (Pacific Press: Mountain View, CA, 1963) p. 11.
[10] Spalding, p. 271.
[11] *Ibid*, p. 307–308.
[12] Cooper, Emma Howell *The Great Advent Movement* (Review & Herald Publishing Assn.: Washington, D.C., 1968) p. 56.
[13] White, Ellen G. *Testimonies for the Church*, Vol. 8 (Pacific Press: Mountain View, CA, 1948) p. 236–237.

Chapter 6

[1] Spalding, Arthur W. *Origin and History of Seventh-day Adventists*, Vol. I (Review & Herald Publishing Assn.: Washington, D.C., 1961) p. 282.
[2] White, Ellen G. *Testimonies for the Church*, Vol. I (Pacific Press: Mountain View, CA, 1948) p. 602. This is a letter from Loughborough, quoted by Ellen G. White.

[3] Spalding, p. 288.

[4] Spalding, Arthur W. *Origin and History of Seventh-day Adventists*, Vol. II (Review & Herald Publishing Assn.: Washington, D.C., 1962) p. 146.

[5] Spalding, Vol. I, p. 208.

[6] *Ibid*, p. 209.

[7] Spalding, Vol. II, p. 203.

[8] Spalding, Vol. I, p. 212.

[9] *Ibid*, p. 213.

Chapter 7

[1] Falkner, Leonard *For Jefferson and Liberty* (Alfred A. Knopf: New York, 1972) p. 63.

[2] Spalding, Arthur W. *Origin and History of Seventh-day Adventists*, Vol. I (Review & Herald Publishing Assn.: Washington, D.C., 1961) p. 315–316.

[3] White, Ellen G. *Testimonies for the Church*, Vol. I (Pacific Press: Mountain View, CA, 1948) p. 356.

[4] Spalding, Vol. I, p. 315.

[5] White, Ellen G. *Testimony Treasures*, Vol. 3 (Pacific Press: Mountain View, CA, 1949) p. 223.

[6] Spalding, Arthur W. (Origin and History of Seventh-day Adventists, Vol. II (Review & Herald Publishing Assn.: Washington, D.C., 1962) p. 171.

[7] Spalding, Vol. II, p. 172.

[8] *Ibid*.

[9] White, *Testimony Treasures*, Vol. 3, p. 220.

[10] Spalding, Vol. II, p. 228–229.

[11] Cooper, Emma Howell *The Great Advent Movement* (Review & Herald Publishing Assn.: Washington, D.C., 1968) p. 174.

[12] Spalding, Vol. II, p. 305.

[13] *Ibid*.

[14] Ibid, p. 306.

[15] *Ibid*, p. 308–309.

Chapter 8

[1] Cooper, Emma Howell *The Great Advent Movement* (Review & Herald Publishing Assn.: Washington, D.C., 1968) p. 81.

[2] *Review and Herald*, 16 April 1872, p. 144.

[3] *Review and Herald*, 7 May 1872, p. 168.

[4] White, Ellen G. *Testimony Treasures*, Vol. 1 (Pacific Press: Mountain View, CA, 1949) p. 570.

[5] *Review and Herald*, 18 March 1873.

[6] Spalding, Arthur W. *Origin and History of Seventh-day Adventists*, Vol. II (Review & Herald Publishing Assn.: Washington, D.C., 1962) p. 355.

[7] *Ibid*, p. 357–358.

[8] *Ibid*, p. 358.

[9] *Ibid*, p. 360.

[10] *Ibid*, p. 316–364.

[11] White, Ellen G. *Special Testimonies on Education* (Pacific Press: Mountain View, CA, 1949) p. 13.

[12] Spalding, Vol. II, p. 97.

[13] *Ibid*, p. 98.

[14] Schaefer, Richard A. *Legacy* (Pacific Press: Mountain View, CA, 1978) p. 49.

[15] White, Ellen G. *Education* (Pacific Press: Mountain View, CA, 1903) p. 13.

Chapter 9

[1] White, Ellen G. *Testimonies for the Church*, Vol. I (Pacific Press: Mountain View, CA, 1948) p. 222.

[2] Spalding, Arthur W. *Origin and History of Seventh-day Adventists*, Vol. I (Review & Herald Publishing Assn.: Washington, D.C., 1961) p. 340.

[3] White, *Testimonies*, Vol. I, p. 485, 492–493.

[4] Cooper, Emma Howell *The Great Advent Movement* (Review & Herald Publishing Assn.: Washington, D.C., 1968) p. 98.

[5] Spalding, Vol. I, p. 369.

[6] Schaefer, Richard A. *Legacy* (Pacific Press: Mountain View, CA, 1978) p. 54.

[7] Robinson, D.E. *The Story of Our Health Message*, 3rd ed. (Southern Publishing Assn.: Nashville, Tenn., 1965) p. 293.

[8] Schaefer, p. 55–56.

[9] *Ibid*, p. 67.

[10] *Ibid*, p. 80.

[11] Spalding, Arthur W. *Origin and History of Seventh-day Adventists*, Vol. III (Review & Herald: Washington, D.C., 1962) p. 141.

[12] Cooper, p. 99.

[13] White, Ellen G. *Testimony Treasures*, Vol. 3 (Pacific Press: Mountain View, CA, 1949) p. 366, 367.

[14] White, *Testimonies*, Vol. I, p. 493.

Chapter 10

[1] Spalding, Arthur W. *Origin and History of Seventh-day Adventists*, Vol. III (Review & Herald Publishing Assn.: Washington, D.C., 1962) p. 19.

[2] *Ibid*, p. 20.

[3] Cooper, Emma Howell *The Great Advent Movement* (Review & Herald Publishing Assn.: Washington, D.C., 1968) p. 60.

[4] Spalding, Vol. III, p. 75.

[5] *Ibid*, p. 77.

[6] *Ibid*, p. 225.

[7] Cooper, p. 93.

[8] Spalding, Vol. III, p. 125.

Chapter 11

[1] Spalding, Arthur W. *Origin and History of Seventh-day Adventists*, Vol. III (Review & Herald Publishing Assn.: Washington, D.C., 1962) p. 248.

[2] Cooper, Emma Howell *The Great Advent Movement* (Re-

view & Herald Publishing Assn.: Washington, D.C., 1968) p. 68.

[3] *Ibid.*

[4] *Seventh-day Adventist Yearbook, 1987* (Review & Herald Publishing Assn.: Hagerstown, MD, 1987) p. 545–557.

[5] Cooper, p. 125.

[6] *Ibid*, p. 129.

[7] *Ibid.*

[8] White, Ellen G. *Testimony Treasures*, Vol. 2 (Pacific Press: Mountain View, CA, 1949) p. 372.

Chapter 12

[1] White, Ellen G. *Testimonies for the Church*, Vol. VII (Pacific Press: Mountain View, CA, 1948) p. 102.

[2] Spalding, Arthur W. *Origin and History of Seventh-day Adventists*, Vol. III (Review & Herald Publishing Assn.: Washington, D.C., 1962) p. 160.

[3] *Ibid*, p. 156.

[4] Schaefer, Richard A. *Legacy* (Pacific Press: Mountain View, CA, 1978) p. 89.

[5] *Ibid*, p. 165.

[6] *Ibid*, p. 92.

[7] *Ibid*, p. 117.

[8] *Ibid*, p. 118.

[9] *Ibid*, p. 124.

[10] *Ibid*, p. 124–125.

[11] *Ibid*, p. 125.

[12] *Ibid*, p. 127.

[13] Telephone interview with Richard A. Schaefer, November 20, 1987.

[14] *Ibid.*

[15] *Ibid.*

[16] Press Release: "A Breakthrough in the Control of Cancer" Loma Linda University Medical Center News Service (Loma Linda University: Loma Linda, CA, 1987) p. 2.

[17]Telephone interview with Richard A. Schaefer.

[18]White, Ellen G. *Testimonies for the Church*, Vol. I (Pacific Press: Mountain View, CA, 1948) p. 493.

Chapter 13

[1]White, Ellen G. *Testimonies for the Church*, Vol. I (Pacific Press: Mountain View, CA, 1948) p. 62.

[2]*Seventh-day Adventist Yearbook, 1987* (Review & Herald Publishing Assn.: Hagerstown, MD, 1987) p. 4.

[3]Durand, Eugene F. *The Story of the Seventh-day Adventist Church* (Review & Herald Publishing Assn.: Hagerstown, MD, 1986) p. 3.

[4]"Structure of the Church," *About the Seventh-day Adventists* (Channing L. Bete Co.: South Deerfield, MA, 1985) p. 11.

[5]*Yearbook*, p. 15.

[6]*Ibid*, p. 15–36.

[7]White, Ellen G. *Testimony Treasures*, Vol. 2 (Pacific Press: Mountain View, CA, 1949) p. 458.

[8]*Yearbook*, p. 4.

[9]White, *Testimony Treasures*, Vol. 2, p. 156.

[10]*Yearbook*, p. 4.

[11]*Ibid.*

[12]Walton, Lewis R. & Herbert E. Douglass *How to Survive the '80s* (Pacific Press: Mountain View, CA, 1982) p. 9–10.

[13]*Yearbook*, p. 8.

Bibliography

About the Seventh-day Adventists Channing L. Bete Co., Inc.: South Deerfield, MA, 1985.

Cable, Mary & the editors of *American Heritage American Manners and Morals* American Heritage Publishing Co.: New York, 1969.

Carmen, Harry J., Harold C. Syrett & Bernard W. Wishy *A History of the American People*, Vol. II Alfred A. Knopf: New York, 1967.

Coffey, Cecil *The Church God Built* Review & Herald Publishing Assn.: Washington, D.C., 1972.

Cooper, Emma Howell *The Great Advent Movement* Review & Herald Publishing Assn.: Washington, D.C., 1968.

Devens, R.M. *Our First Century* C.A. Nichols & Co.: Springfield, MA, 1876.

Durand, Eugene F. *The Story of the Seventh-day Adventist Church* Review & Herald Publishing Assn.: Hagerstown, MD, 1986.

Falkner, Leonard *For Jefferson and Liberty: The United States in War and Peace, 1800–1815* Alfred A. Knopf: New York, 1972.

Katz, William L. *Eyewitness: The Negro in American History* Pitman Publishing Corp.: New York, 1968.

Maxwell, C. Mervyn *Tell It to the World* Pacific Press: Mountain View, CA, 1977.

Miller, Douglas T. *Then Was the Future: The North in the Age of Jackson, 1815–1850* Alfred A. Knopf: New York, 1973.

Review and Herald Review & Herald Publishing Assn.: Battle Creek, MI, 16 April 1872.

Review and Herald Review & Herald Publishing Assn.: Battle Creek, MI, 7 May 1872.

Robinson, D.E. *The Story of Our Health Message: The Origin, Character, and Development of Health Education in the Seventh-day Adventist Church*, 3rd ed. Southern Publishing Assn.: Nashville, TN, 1965.

Schaefer, Richard A. *Legacy: The Heritage of a Unique International Medical Outreach* Pacific Press: Mountain View, CA, 1978.

Sellers, Charles & Henry May *A Synopsis of American History* Rand McNally: Chicago, 1963.

Seventh-day Adventist Yearbook, 1987 Review & Herald Publishing Assn.: Hagerstown, MD, 1987.

Spalding, Arthur W. *Origin and History of Seventh-day Adventists*, Vols I–IV Review & Herald Publishing Assn.: Washington, D.C, 1961, 1962.

The Telescope Bond Astronomical Club: Cambridge, MA, October 1934.

Trim, Marye *"Tell Me About Ellen White"* Review & Herald Publishing Assn.: Washington, D.C., 1975.

Utt, Richard *A Century of Miracles* Pacific Press: Mountain View, Ca, 1963.

Walton, Lewis R. & Herbert E. Douglass *How to Survive the '80s* Pacific Press: Mountain View, CA, 1982.

White, Ellen G. *Education* Pacific Press: Mountain View, CA, 1903.

——— *Special Testimonies on Education* Pacific Press: Mountain View, CA, 1949.

——— *Testimonies for the Church* Vols. I, VII, VIII Pacific Press: Mountain View, CA, 1948.

——— *Testimony Treasures*, Vols. 1–3 Pacific Press: Mountain View, CA, 1949.

Other Sources

Press Release: "*A Breakthrough in the Control of Cancer: Loma Linda University Medical Center to be First Hospital Using a Proton Beam Accelerator for Patient Treatment*" Loma Linda University Medical Center News Service: Loma Linda, CA 1987.

Press Release: "*A Breakthrough in the Control of Cancer: Proton Therapy Advances and the Control of Cancer at Loma Linda*" Loma Linda University Medical Center News Service: Loma Linda, CA, 1987.

Telephone interview with Richard A. Schaefer, Community Relations, Loma Linda University Medical Center, Loma Linda, CA, November 20, 1987.

Index